LONG DISTANCE
FLYER, G-EBFO

Kenneth T. Ward

LONG DISTANCE FLYER, G-EBFO

"Registered with the IP Rights Office Copyright Registration Service Ref:
4748692944"

Published by Kenneth T. Ward
Publishing partner: Paragon Publishing, Rothersthorpe
© Kenneth T. Ward 2016

ISBN 978-1-78222-456-3
Book design, layout and production management by Into Print
www.intoprint.net
+44 (0)1604 832149

Contents

Foreword

This is an exciting story based on an historical event. Familiar as Alan Cobham was with long distance flights, the idea of flying from England to Australia and back in a small seaplane offered a new and dangerous adventure, added to which he wanted to experience flying in the Monsoon period, so testing the route during the worst weather.

Sergeant Arthur Ward, my Uncle, an engine mechanic in the Royal Air Force, became Alan Cobham's flight engineer for the flight to Australia and back to England. He agreed to take the place of the engineer Arthur Elliott, Cobham's regular flight engineer, who was killed in Iraq. Ward and Elliott were important for helping the pilot Cobham prove to a disinterested British Government that long distance, commercial flights, to the other side of the World were possible and important for bringing the Dominions closer.

Alan Cobham who was presented with a Knighthood, by King Gorge the Fifth, after the flight had come a long way from his Veterinary days as an infantryman in charge of sick horses, during the early parts of the 1914–1918 Great War. He volunteered to join the Royal Flying Corps, later to become the Royal Air Force, after being inspired by the flying machines that were flown over his head towards the battle lines during the last days of the war. He applied, was accepted and trained to fly the military aircraft available at that time. (See Cobham The Flying Years- by Colin Cruddas)

Some of the diary events of Sir Alan Cobham in his book, 'Australia and Back' published in 1927 by R & C Black (Out of print, now reproduced as "To the ends of the earth,' published by Tempus Publishing 2007) is useful in confirming what happened in parts of the journey. The Times reported, sometimes weekly, on the journey and this is in the Public Domain. In 1926 Aviation Safety Network reported that, in the world, 221 aircraft crashed and were written off. It was a risky occupation to be a pilot at that time.

Kenneth T Ward. DipM FCIM.

OCT.1 (260) LONDON ROCHESTER-JUNE 30
SEPT.30 (780) PARIS
SEPT.29 (830) ORBETELLO
NAPLES (1200) JUNE 30
SEPT.28 (800) ATHENS (900) JULY 1
SEPT.27 (850) ALEXANDRETTA
BAGHDAD (1350) JULY 4
SEPT.26 (820) BASRA (300) JULY 6
BUSHIRE (250) JULY 13
BANDAR ABBAS (420) JULY 14
SEPT.23 (200) JASK
SEPT.24 (420) CHARBAR
SEPT.25 (800) KARACHI (770) JULY 18

Sir Alan C
Leader a

Cyril S. Capel
Melbourne — London

The end of the flight Westminster Oct.1st 1926

Cobham K.B.E.,A.F.C.
and organiser of the expedition

The De Havilland Type 50 Seaplane, engine 385 H.P.
Armstrong Siddeley "Jaguar"
Leaving Rochester June 30 1926

The late Arthur Bullar Elliott
Died of wounds Basra July 7 1926

RAWALPUR (500) JULY 20
DELHI (400) JULY 21
T.21 (550) ALLAHABAD (400) JULY 22
SEPT.19 (440) CALCUTTA (550) JULY 23
SEPT.14 (500) AKYAB (440) JULY 24
SEPT.15 (500) RANGOON (500) JULY 25
(400) VICTORIA PT. (350) JULY 27
(350) PENANG (400) JULY 28
SINGAPORE (400) JULY 29
(800) MUNTOK (250) JULY 31
BATAVIA (350) AUG 1
PT. 3 (500) SOURABAYA (450) AUG.2
BIMA (450) AUG 3
SEPT.4 (500) KUPANG (550) AUG.4
SEPT.2 (180) PORT DARWIN (500) AUG.5
SEPT.1 (700) KATHERINE
NEWCASTLE WATERS (400) AUG.8
CAMOUWEAL (400) AUG.9
AUG31 (500) ALICE SPRINGS
CHARLEVILLE (750) AUG.10
AUG30 (25) OODNADATTA
SYDNEY (JAS) AUG.11
AUG29 (400) ADELAIDE
MELBOURNE (500) AUG.15

Sergt A.H. Ward R.A.F.
Basra — Melbourne — London

I wish to thank the Royal Airforce Museum's Archive section for their great help in providing photographs and information essential for completing this book.
Ken Ward

1: Sir Sefton Brancker

Four years before his untimely death in the Airship 101 that caught fire in the early hours of 5th October 1930 near Beauvais, France, Air Marshal Sir Sefton Brancker was an important personality in the history of British Civil and Military aviation. He was trained at Woolwich, where he joined the Royal Artillery. He served in South Africa and India, where he made his first flight in 1910. He held administrative posts in the Royal Flying Corps, and later in the Royal Air Force during World War One. He received his Knighthood in 1919 and became an Air Vice-Marshall shortly after.

In 1924 Brancker was Chairman of the Royal Aero Club (RAeC) Racing Committee and his dynamic leadership led to the RAeC forming the Light Aero Club in 1925, which helped UK clubs to be provided with new and improved aircraft, such as the de Havilland Moth.

It was in this period that Sir Sefton came to know Alan Cobham, who had won the Kings Cup Air Race in 1924, at his third attempt. Cobham was chosen to accompany Brancker, who became the British Director of Civil Aviation, to India and Burma. The purpose of the visit was to assess the viability of setting up airship routes to the Far East. However, on their return, Brancker was of the opinion that the aeroplane and not the airship would eventually win the day.

The return journey from India and Burma was completed in March 1925 using the de Havilland D.H.50 Bi-plane aircraft with the registration letters G-EBFO or known as "FO" for short, equipped with a Puma 240hp engine and it was this aircraft, but with a new Armstrong 385hp Jaguar radial engine, that Cobham completed another long journey to South Africa and back in November 1925 despite the occasional forced landing,.

Cobham's flight engineer Arthur Elliott became his regular engineer having flown with Cobham both to India and South Africa. The latter journey was to prove that Imperial Airways could start a regular air route to South Africa and it is rumoured that the Company provided a contribution of £500 to ensure that any photographs of the flight showed the Imperial Airways emblem on the side of "FO". Imperial Airways was formed on 31 March 1924 by the merger of Scott-Paines British Marine Air Navigation Company and three other airlines.

In 1925 aircraft were being used locally in many countries of the world but international air travel on a commercial basis from continent to continent hardly existed. Cobham was of the opinion that connecting the Dominions of the British Empire by air was essential. However, for most of the journey airfields or landing strips were often not available and if aircraft were used locally in other countries they were delivered by ship, not flown there, and an airstrip would be prepared after receiving the aircraft.

Cobham had been the test pilot for Geoffrey de Havilland's new Company that started in 1920 after the company Airco, where de Havilland worked, went into liquidation having been bought by the Birmingham Small Arms Company at the end of the First World War. When they found that the Company was in a bad state financially, caused by the cessation of hostilities that did not require so many aircraft, BSA decided to liquidate. Geoffrey de Havilland, with the help of the previous Airco owner, Mr Holt Thomas, purchased from the Liquidator the stock and machinery and other assets to continue making the DH aircraft originally designed by Geoffrey de Havilland for Airco Industries.

Sir Stefton Branker, who had wanted the British Government to take an interest in long distance air travel to bring the dominions closer in travel time, also wanted to give Britain the lead in International Air Travel and worked hard to secure political backing. In 1926 flying machines, delivered by ship, were used for local travel in many parts of the World for securing borders, mail distribution, local land surveying, doctors, business and political work, military and police use. Long distance intercontinental flying was not known.

2: Mrs Gladys Cobham

Ninety years ago, at home in Buckland Crescent, London NW3, Alan Cobham and his wife Gladys set about raising money for a flight to Australia and back and to secure permission for the various stops on route. Now it was for Cobham and Elliott to prove it would be possible to reach Australia and return to Great Britain by air.

Their trusted de Havilland aircraft was to be used again, but be converted into a seaplane or if required be changed back into a land aircraft. The formalities for future regular long distance passenger air routes would be worked out later but at this time Cobham considered that seaplanes would be the carrier.

Alan Cobham had married the actress and opera singer, Miss Gladys Lloyd, on 30th June 1922 after a whirlwind courtship, because he always had to save precious time for flying. He had a promise of marriage within a week of their first meeting.

Gladys had appeared in a touring review but following her marriage to Alan Cobham his frenetic lifestyle was to take her over and every day correspondence amounted to a tremendous amount of work. In the four years since being married and also giving birth to their son Geoffrey, getting landing and mooring permission with each Government of the countries en route required a mountain of paperwork. Additionally there was a lot of correspondence to clear up from the previous journey to Cape Town.

Long distance flying was now in Alan Cobham's blood and in order to impress on an indifferent Government administration he decided to fly from Rochester in Kent, England, to Melbourne in Australia and back to London and deliver a petition to Parliament.

Gladys Cobham had recalled how easy it was to raise funds for the last journey to South Africa but it was proving difficult to raise finance for the planned flight to Australia and back to England.

Alan Cobham would reply that he considered about 20 per cent of a flight was down to the trivial matter of handling the control lever and rudder bar of the pilot's cockpit, whereas the backbone of the successful flight will always be the ground organisation that is put in before the flight commenced and would continue throughout a journey.

It was important, to get the backers and sponsors involved, as finance was essential to make payments along the route. However the departure date was also important, for although Cobham wanted to assure interested parties that flying through a Monsoon presented few problems, in practice their plans would involve trying to avoid the worse of the monsoon weather, if possible, and therefore he wanted to leave as soon was possible.

There was not enough time to have all stages of the route paid for by the backers and sponsors in advance of the departure date, therefore Cobham decided to give lectures or after dinner speeches to raise funds before departure and also to do the same during the journey, whenever possible, by charging for his services. A lot of the finance therefore would only arrive after their departure apart from the cash in hand obtained from his speeches.

Never the less they had a few promises. Sir Charles Wakefield, for example, of the Castrol Oil Company wanted to be a big sponsor and a successful flight for him would be good for his Company profile.

Because Cobham was monitoring the modifications to the aircraft with the de Havilland Aircraft Company and the Short Brothers Rochester Sea Plane Factory, as floats would be added to what was a ground landing aircraft, it was Gladys who took on the task of sending out letters and cables to the various stops on route. Alan Cobham knew the stops required when he had flown to India and back but they were made on land based landing strips and the flight to Australia and back would be made in a seaplane because of the difficulty with purpose made aerodromes after India. The re-fuelling stops on water and address details were supplied by the fuel suppliers and helped by the British Government Overseas Department, which sometimes had an Embassy or Consulate in the refuelling stop country.

Stanley Baldwin's Conservative Government had only just avoided bringing England to a standstill over the General Strike and the Politicians were relatively uninterested in Cobham's plan in 1926. They were only interested in reaching the summer recess and relaxing away from Parliamentary frolics.

However, the Times Newspaper reported a letter received from Sir Samuel Hoare, Secretary of State for Air, 'Best wishes for a speedy and successful journey. Your flight should furnish further convincing proof in the part aviation is to play in breaking down the barriers of time and distance and so linking the overseas Dominions still more closely with our country.' Here was one politician who took the intending flight seriously.

The flight from South Africa using the new Jaguar 385 engine had been a success and the aircraft "FO" was transported to Rochester on the Medway, where at the factory of Short Brothers it was to have metal floats fixed for the flight to Australia and back. It was planned that the floats would be taken off the aircraft in Darwin and replaced by wheels where landing on land was probably not a problem.

Cobham had less than five months to plan the journey, arrange for local support at each stop and get sponsors. The principal sponsor, Sir Charles Wakefield of the Castrol Oil Company, arranged to have his name painted on each side of the aircraft below the windows of the forward cabin. The flight became known as 'The Charles Wakefield Flight to Australia'.

Gladys and Alan Cobham set to work sending letters and cables to the various authorities in each port of call to arrange for moorings, accommodation and refuelling by one of the three Oil Companies supporting the flight.

There were to be more than fifty planned stops for the round journey and the organisation necessary to contact and receive replies to their correspondence was a most time consuming passion. Gladys took on this work gladly for she so admired her husband's work enormously that her profession as an opera singer and actress had to be abandoned. She was a mother now anyway and that and work for her husband used up her time.

Familiar as Cobham was with long distance flights the idea of flying from England to Australia and back with a seaplane offered a new adventure, something different to anything that had been attempted before. From Calcutta to Australia, for example, it was simply impossible to land anywhere except on a specially prepared aerodrome and these were generally not available. He did not relish being caught out in a severe monsoon over such country, or over jungle, or over water for that matter but with no prospects of landing on an airfield he decided that a seaplane offered many advantages provided his course stayed close to water.

In the year 1919 the problem with landing strips was reported, when crews of six aircraft attempted the first flight from England to Australia. The Australian Prime Minister, the Right Honourable Billy Hughes, impressed by the huge potential for aviation, offered, on behalf of the Commonwealth, a prize of ten thousand pounds to the winner of a competition to complete the flight within thirty days. The rules were the crew had to be Australian, however, a Frenchman by the name of Etienne Poulet, departed ahead of the other six aircraft, but had to withdraw at Moulmein, Burma owing to engine problems.

The first Australian entry to depart was the Vickers Vimy bi-plane aircraft G-EAOU powered by two Rolls-Royce Eagle eight engines, each three hundred and sixty horsepower, and commanded by Captain Ross Smith, his brother Lieutenant Keith Smith as Navigator and co-pilot, and mechanics, Sergeants Bennett and Shiers. The aircraft was designed during the 1914-18 Great War, as a heavy bomber. The span of the wings was nearly seventy feet and length of the fuselage was forty-three feet and it stood fifteen feet off the ground. Spare parts for the flight had to be carried inside the aircraft, as it was impossible to have them shipped out in time. This added considerably to the weight and was offset by not including a wireless or personal items.

The route had been planned in four stages and fuel supplies were sent to remote landing areas, some of these eventually proved to be non-existent or too difficult for landing. They took off from Hounslow on 12th November in dense fog, and bad weather followed their flight that at one time at nine thousand feet, flying over Lyon in southern France, snow entered their open cockpits and they experienced great pain from the cold and from the ninety miles an hour wind. (See "The First Flight to Australia, 'London to Port Darwin in Twenty-Eight Days in an Open Cockpit,' " by H.G.Castle. Also airwaysmuseum.com.)

Many problems existed during the air-race to Australia. Landing strips were proving to be a problem and several stops resulted in getting bogged down in deep mud. Sometimes landing on a remote beach was the only way to get down, and it took hours, if not days to get the fuel to the aircraft when they could not use the planned landing area. The Smith brothers and crew were declared the winners, but the other aircraft in the competition had varying fortune and did not arrive, except the Airco DH9 (fore-runner of the DH 50) flown by Lt Paul Parer and Lt McIntosh, who left Hounslow on 8th January 1920 and arrived at Darwin on 2nd August, some two hundred and six days later. They received five hundred pounds each for their endurance, although way outside the time limit for the race rules.

Alan Cobham continued the task to conduct lectures and meetings to enthuse potential sponsors about his journey and the reasons why it should be made, and would continue this task along the journey to Melbourne.

3: Flying with floats for the first time

Cobham and his flight engineer, Elliott, arrived at the Short Brothers Rochester works a few days before they were due to depart on the first stage of their flight.

In 1900 Eustace Short and his brother Oswald Short visited the Paris Exposition (World Trade Fair) where they saw how to manufacture balloons for carrying man and decided to produce their own, to offer for sale. When they persuaded their other brother Horace to join them, in 1909, upon hearing of the success of Wright Brothers demonstration of their airplane in Paris, the Brothers decided that the balloon was not the way ahead and the airplane was the future. They obtained the rights to produce the Wright Brothers design in Britain and started to produce it in 1909 and by the outbreak of World War One they were producing their own designs for both successful landplanes and seaplanes, with over 900 Short S.184 seaplanes being produced. (See Wikipedia, Short Brothers.).

Cobham and Elliott preparing for departure.

G-EBFO, their aircraft, lay bobbing in the water, just off of the main ramp, used by Short Brothers to wheel down flying boats from the factory into the river. Known as 'FO', it had been renovated after the flight to Cape Town and back. Cobham sat in the cockpit having climbed aboard in an undignified manner using the float and two steps in the side of the aircraft to climb up.

He sat motionless for a while. He thought about the engine, which had behaved perfectly on the flight to South Africa and back to England. It had fourteen cylinders, compression ratio five to one and powered by the new KLG Spark Plugs, (Invented by Mr.Kenelm Lee Guiness), and it was normally rated 385 British Horse Power at 1700 revolutions per minute with a maximum 1870 R.P.M producing 400 B.H.P., at maximum speed. The petrol consumption on the South African flight used 19 to 20 gallons each hour (Approximately 70 litres per hour). The Oil consumption used half a gallon each hour (Nearly 2 litres each hour).

His left hand passed over the leather trim around the cockpit edge that had been replaced since he had last flown "F.O." He looked down at the floats that had been fixed to replace the wheel undercarriage. They protruded a long way forward of the front of the aircraft so as to balance it on a level plain when on the water. Cobham had not flown using floats before, never the less, he thought there would be no problem getting the aircraft off the water even if it would be different from flying a land-based aircraft. In fact the usual take-off procedure to push the joystick forward to raise the tail during the run on the runway was the opposite that was required for seaplanes as the floats would dig in and stop the aircraft.

In front of him was the joystick, topped by a leather-covered oval grip, by which the aircraft would be steered using his hands, in conjunction with the rudder bar controlled by his feet. The Elevators on either side of the rudder wings at the back of the aircraft controlled the pitch when the joystick was pushed forward or pulled back.

Ailerons on the bi-plane wings controlled the roll when the joystick was pushed to either side and the rudder controlled direction by pushing on the foot controls, left pedal to turn left and right pedal for right direction. These controls were particularly important because the forward view was very limited and he was required to roll the aircraft from side to side when landing to gain a controlled and visual approach to the airfield or the water if floats were connected to the aircraft.

Pre-flight inspection always included the following: Cobham pushed the joystick forward and back and looked back to the tail section each time to see the elevator flaps on the rear tail-plane wings move up or down and in flight would either lift the nose or drop it forward. Next he moved the joystick from side to side and looked over the side to see the ailerons, which were hinged on each wing, move in opposite directions.

When the joystick was pushed to the left, the left side ailerons turned up and the right side aileron turned down and this would make the aircraft roll to the left. The opposite happened when the joystick was pushed to the right, with the right side ailerons turning up and the left side turning down. The operation was controlled via cables attached on four sides to a fulcrum that was fixed to a ball and socket, and this was connected to the joystick. A rod connecting the lower aileron with the upper aileron, on each wing, kept the ailerons parallel.

The rudder was tested by using his feet to move the rudder bar that had cables attached and fed back on the outside of the aircraft to the rudder at the rear, similar to the cables for the elevator flaps. Half way up on the rudder there were small pre-set flaps to adjust for direction deviation caused by the rotation of the propeller.

When the joystick was used the ailerons provided roll and used in conjunction with the rudder, helped turn the aircraft. Pushing the left side of the rudder bar with his left foot turned the rudder to the left. The opposite happened when Cobham pushed the rudder bar with his right foot.

He observed the wings now gleaming after having the linen covering re-doped, that was necessary following the battering given to "FO" by the elements on that long journey to Cape Town and back. Under the canvass of each wing lay the delicate assembly of plywood and spruce made up into a hollow frame, light in weight but very strong. The surface shape of the wings controlled lifting the aircraft into the air. They were flat underneath each wing but on the top of each wing gently shaped in an upward curve high in the centre tailoring off towards the rear to push the airflow up. The principle was that air flowing over this wing shape would create a vacuum on the top of the wing and the pressure under the wing would keep the aircraft in the air.

Above the pilot dividing the top wing, was the petrol tank, of an aerodynamic design with a large rounded 'Bull nose' at the front and tailored to a thin section at the rear. There was a stop cock immediately under the tank to isolate the flow of fuel when the aircraft was moored. When the valve was open the fuel would fall by gravity through a tube down to the carburettor of the engine where the fuel would be distributed into one of the piston combustion chambers situated around the radius of the engine.

The aircraft carried about one hundred and fifty gallons of fuel (about 680 litres), some in the top tank dividing the wings and the rest inside the cabin in a tank connected to a hand pump that the engineer, on being instructed by the pilot who had a fuel gauge in the cockpit, would manually pump the fuel into the top tank. An electric pump was considered too heavy for the flight. This tank would be filled using a funnel, inside the cabin. There was a stop- cock valve on top of the manual pump to stop evaporation.

Separating the wings were four wooden inter-struts on each side fitted with ball and cup, and to tie everything together were cables, tensioned and tied across between the wings, rather like cross thread-ing of shoe laces to hold the inter-struts in place. The tail assembly made up of the rudder and tail wings were also made of strong mate-rials, similar to the wings but were reinforced with metal rods. The fuselage was made from waterproofed canvas on a strong metal frame that enclosed the cabin, and was joined to the metal bracket assembly holding the Jaguar radial engine. The tail section was connected to the fuselage frame.

The airspeed indicator fixed to the port side forward wing strut was made from a metal spring with a white paddle that would be forced back by the air at speed. A calibrated scale situated behind the paddle would indicate to the pilot important information, but a variable resistance hinged with the paddle also sent information to a cockpit instrument, made by Smith & sons (M.A.) Ltd, and the information gave the pilot the opportunity to lift the aircraft off the ground at a pre-determined speed and to perform other manoeuvres when airbourne..

The really important piece of aircraft equipment, however proved to be the compass and Cobham used the finest aeroplane compass in the world at that time. It was known as the Hughes Aperiodic and was the result of exhaustive mathematical research and experiment in the latter part of the 1914-1918 World War One.

Inside the body of a similar aircraft showing the spare fuel tank.

Actual photograph of Mr Alan Cobham's DH.50 'J' Dashboard

The cockpit of the DeHavilland DH50 J that Mr Alan Cobham flew, with the compass in the fore-ground, the hatch to communicate with the forward cabin at the top of the picture and an array of important control instruments supplied by Smith and Son (M.A.) Ltd. (Later, 'Smith Industries'.)

The Instruments were listed as follows:
1. Engine speed Indicator.
2. Oil Pressure Gauge.
3. Upper main Fuel Tank contents Gauge.
4. Oil Temperature Gauge.
5. Air Speed Indicator Gauge.
6. Inclinometers (a) Cross level (b) Fore and Aft levels.
7. Height Indicator (Altimeter).
8. Hughes Aperiodic Compass.
9. Watch.

The second most important equipment was the helmet that had to withstand the force of winds of 120 miles per hour and engine noise. Cobham preferred one similar to that made by the American Company of Spalding with ear pockets that could be filled with cotton wool. On occasion he would also wear earplugs made by Elliott's or those of Edward Baum manufacture.

When the helmet strap was pulled tight under the chin the helmet was sealed around the face so keeping out the force of the air and keeping the ear pockets close to the ears.

Elliott's job would always be to conduct engine tests according to the Aircraft Servicing Schedule that included checking the valve springs, replenish oil and fuel, also check the various cables connecting to the aircraft controls and wing bracing wires, check airframe covering material, the propeller (And there were two more propellers stored under the fuselage as spares), engine exterior for oil leaks, rectify defects and notify the pilot, before take off.

Cobham shouted to Elliott that he should give 'FO' several take off and landings on the water, to get used to the addition of the floats. Elliott who had arrived to conduct an inspection informed him that although he had commenced a pre-flight inspection earlier, he still needed to complete the service routine, which he would also do after each flight.

When Cobham had completed several take offs and landings on

the water they both took on board several items for the journey. The aircraft was by now several pounds heavier than when conducting the practice runs. Each airman then left to wait the departure day and the aircraft was taken out of the water and put into the factory.

Three Oil Companies had been organised to supply the fuel for "FO". The British Petroleum Company was to supply B.P. Spirit from London to Charbar, the Burma Oil Company from Karachi to Rangoon, the Shell Mex Company from Victoria Point to the Dutch East Indies and on from Darwin to Melbourne. The return journey was mapped out similarly with a few changes. All of these Companies were delighted to sponsor and be involved, as long distance air travel would grow their Companies in the future.

Taking off on water involved a different procedure to avoid pushing the floats under.

4: "The first day" to Naples

The date of departure was postponed three times for various reasons. On the last day of June 1926 Cobham, exactly four years to the day since he and Gladys were married, was called from his bed at 04.00 hours in the "Bull Hotel" in Rochester, so that he and Elliott, who was already tucking into a hearty breakfast, could fly to Naples in one day. Cobham had said goodbye to his wife the day before and then motored down to prepare for the flight.

Elliott, Lord Wakefield, major sponsor and Cobham, on morning of departure, outside of the Short Brothers works.

After having a full English breakfast also, Alan Cobham and Arthur Elliott were ready to have 'FO' rolled down the slope to the water. A photo session had been arranged for Lord Wakefiled to use as advertising for the Castrol Oil Company he owned and eventually they left Rochester from the River Medway at 05.30 hours on the 30th June 1926. There was not a breath of wind to help them get off the calm water. The aircraft was over weight, Cobham knew that the maximum permissible load of a De Havilland DH50J aircraft is four thousand two hundred pounds but owing to the extra weight of the floats and other equipment such as spare petrol and small wheels and spindle for the floats, the maximum load was now in the region of five thousand pounds. A wireless was left out to save weight, and anyway would have been useless for many parts of the journey.

However, despite the extra weight, Cobham managed to get airborne and turned gradually as they climbed to wave to the crowd that now included his wife and many of their friends, who had travelled down from west London in the early hours of the morning to see them off.

Shortly, after they left Rochester they passed over Maidstone at a speed of about 100 miles per hour (160 Kilometers per hour), at a cruising height of between 2000 to 3000 thousand feet (600 to 900 meters) on a compass course for Rouen, France, and at Hastings passed over the English Channel. Cobham was not a seaplane pilot and with the exception of a few trial flights prior to their departure, he had never flown a seaplane before. Likewise his engineer, Arthur Elliott knew little about using water as a runway.

They journeyed to Marseilles following various rivers, entering France at Rouen where they turned southeast, flying along the course of the Seine towards Sartrouville, a French seaplane base on the Seine north of Paris where they had arranged to refill, if necessary.

Cobham had estimated that with a favourable following wind they would have enough fuel to get them to Marseille from Rochester at about eighteen gallons an hour. On paper the six hundred and seventy miles journey looked to be quite safe with a large margin of petrol but in reality should they meet with a head wind the margin would be small because more fuel would be used each mile.

All the way from Rouen to Paris Cobham tried to calculate on the writing pad in his cockpit, behind the windshield, whether they could reach Marseille without stopping to refill at Sartrouville, and finally he decided to carry on convinced that a northwest wind would prevail throughout the flight and that they would reach Marseille safely.

They passed over Sartrouville, much to the disappointment of the ground crew awaiting the refuelling stop, then over Paris and down the Seine towards Fontainebleau. They then flew over open country following the Loire River for hundreds of miles, eventually flying over St.Etienne.

It was a perfect day and the country below them looked beautiful. At four thousand five hundred feet they flew over the mountains around Mont Pilat and then down to the Rhone valley.

The variable, misty, cold weather of northern Europe started to disappear as they flew over Orange south of Lyon where the colder misty air was replaced by warm, clear air. They landed at the Marignane airbase, near Marseille, at 11.50 am after six hours forty minutes of non-stop flight from Rochester, on the Berre Lake alongside the shores of the land airfield that made both an ideal seaplane and aeroplane base.

There they found that the fuel for "FO" had been left about two miles away from their berth, but after a delay of half an hour the fuel arrived and when refuelled they were on their way again. They left at 2.45pm for Naples. There was an air of security as Cobham opened up the engine and climbed into the air without his customary fear about holes that might be in the surface of the aerodrome or the fact that a tyre might burst, or that telegraph lines might impede the take off, or any other problems attached to an average land aerodrome.

The course from Marseille to Naples continued along the south coast of France, passing over Ile de Porquerolles, in the Iles d'Hyeres a small group of islands off the City of Toulon and out into the

Mediterranean in a south east direction towards the south of Corsica, through the Straits of Bonificio between Corsica and Sardinia. The sea was very clear and they observed shoals of tuna, dolphin and a few whales on this part of the journey.

The area of the Straits of Bonificio is known for a famous disaster which occurred in February 1855, when the French frigate Semillante, on it's way to supply troops for the Crimean war, hit a reef and all 750 soldiers and navy drowned. The Straits are only about 7 miles (11Kms) wide and is a dangerous sea route for larger ships.

Cobham continued over the sea to the coast of Italy, arriving at Naples at 7.45pm. It was a worrying moment for Cobham because he had almost miscalculated the time when the evening got dark. They landed after the sun had set and with only half an hour of semi daylight left.

In future he would carefully check when the sun rose so that sunset could be calculated, because his course took him ever east, against time. Miscalculation was a possibility. However it was necessary to meet at the stopping points as planned.

As he approached Naples Cobham got to thinking about the last time he was in Italy. His thoughts went back to 1921 when Cobham, employed by the DeHavilland Aircraft Company, was the first pilot to be chosen for the first long distance charter flight and flew wealthy American Lucien Sharpe around Europe and the Middle East in a DH9c aircraft. The journey came to an un-ceremonial end when engine failure brought the aircraft down in the main shipping channel in Venice.

The seaplane base at Naples was behind the little island of Nisida, which is a rock about three hundred yards from the mainland upon which is built a prison. A small harbour served as a secure area shared by local seaplanes and small fishing boats.

Nisida

There was a slight problem when landing on the water because of the telegraph wires that spanned the water were several metres in the air,

29

which made for an awkward approach for any seaplane that wanted to land. Never-the-less Cobham had been made aware in London of the hazard but he only narrowly missed them as they were difficult to see in the fading light.

The instant they landed a motor launch came out to meet them carrying some Italian friends of Cobham. They took them in tow to the safe mooring of the small harbour, in preparation for refuelling. Although tired after their journey the refuelling commenced by Elliott using the obsolete method of pouring petrol out of cans into the re-fuelling hole on the top of the tank. Despite the great technical advances in aircraft design Cobham wondered why inefficient, primitive refuelling methods were still wasting valuable time.

Cobham signed for the petrol, received from the British Petroleum Company by their fuel agent, and then with Elliott and some friends he had met on previous flights, went to the mainland in a small boat for dinner. They ate at a restaurant on a small pier that jutted out from the rocks.

Whether it was the long distance travelled on the first day or the meal of the night before, but during the next morning Cobham was indisposed, confessing to feeling unwell, and the departure planned for 5.30am did not take place until he was well enough to travel. The stress of the pre-flight planning maybe had taken an early toll. Meanwhile, Elliott took control of the departure details and pre-flight checks.

The Times reported, July 2ⁿᵈ 'Cobham was taken ill, feeling totally drained with exhaustion. Many days and into the night had been spent arranging the details for the several stops on route and it had made him ill. On July 3ʳᵈ they left Naples for Athens'.

5: A noise in the sky

After a refuelling stop Cobham and Elliott left Athens on 3rd July at 12.15pm and arrived in Alexandretta some 760 miles flying distance. Alexandretta is a town on the edge of the Turkish and Arab worlds and a port city of moderate importance throughout their history. In 1926 it had a small population of Europeans being resident there for centuries.

They were met by the Consular staff and stayed the night at La Maison du Vice-Consul d'Angleterre. The next morning early the metal propeller, fitted at Rochester, was changed and the spare made of wood, that was stored on the aircraft, was fitted. Four propellers were used throughout the journey, one more than they carried was picked up on route in exchange. The metal propeller was stored, slung under the aircraft for use later.

They departed for Baghdad on the 4th July landing on the River Tigris at 7.10pm. Distance 460 miles. They were met by a long boat and taken into toe towards a landing stage.

Members of the Royal Air Force met their aircraft that was immediately surrounded by Air Force buddies of Elliot, some were from his school days, who gladly took over some of his tasks such as refuelling so that the servicing of the aircraft took little time.

Landing on the River Tigris, at Baghdad and met by the RAF launch to take them to a safe mooring.

They had moored close to the British Embassy in front of the Social Club that was sited near the water's edge and this was where a welcoming committee held a reception. One could see the Polo field from here and the stables containing the ponies. It appeared that a game was in progress with six ponies and their riders, three in each team. They were colourful in the team sweaters and the team colours for each of the pony's ankle protectors.

Cobham and Elliot had a good nights sleep in the officers quarters, despite Elliot being entertained by his friends into the early hours of the morning. 'FO' was made ready and was soon lifted into the air by Cobham on 5th July.

Whilst the journey from Rochester had, so far proceeded to plan, as 'FO' was being flown low through a sand storm from Baghdad, at a height of about 50 feet they encountered the first of hostilities. It was not known at the time, but as Cobham flew close to the Tigris River, with difficulty seeing the horizon and about 120 miles from Basra, a lone Arab riding a horse looked up on hearing a sound, took aim and fired his rifle at the 'Noise in the Sky'. The bullet made a piecing sound that shrilled above the sound of the engine. At first Cobham thought there had been an explosion in the cabin, then changed his thoughts to thinking that a wing stay, one of which separated the two wings, had snapped. Instantly Cobham shouted through the connecting tube into the cabin asking Elliott what had happened? Were they on fire he enquired, because his thoughts changed to the possibility that a distress pistol rocket may have exploded?

Elliott replied, but in a low voice, that a petrol pipe had broken, but over the noise of the engine it was very difficult to hear him. Presently, Cobham passed a piece of paper with the question 'What's wrong?' to Elliott through the hatch between the cockpit and the cabin and after a while it was handed back by Elliott indicating that, 'Pipe burst, am bleeding!' It was enough to worry Cobham who wanted to know more? Elliott screamed he was bleeding badly!

Cobham looked through the cabin flap and could just make out Elliott who looked up but with his head at an unusual angle. He knew that Elliott must be seriously wounded as his voice sounded weak and he was gradually slipping down the side of his cabin. Cobham was prepared to land 'FO' on the river but could only just see through the sand storm that produced bad visibility over the flooded plains to the side of a wide River, the River Tigris, necessary for guiding them to Basra. Cobham had no way of knowing how deep the water was for a landing, or if he landed and could not take off again, or whether he could do that single handed running the risk of beaching the aircraft. He shouted through the speaking tube again but Elliott did not respond. He looked through the flap between him and the cabin but could only see the top of Elliott's head.

The heat was terrific and the hot engine was causing concern for Cobham. It was essential that he kept the aircraft going at maximum speed to reach Basra where he knew he could get help. However the loss of blood that Elliott encountered might have been something he, Cobham, could have assisted in stopping. Many alternatives shot through his mind. The River Tigris now became wider as it joined the Euphrates at Shatt-al-Arab. He could now land on the water but it was not long to Basra, and the medical facilities that he knew would help Elliott.

He decided to keep going. It was 110 degrees Fahrenheit (43 Degrees Centigrade) in the shade that day and flying low with the throttle wide open was a problem. Gradually the oil temperature started to rise and as the warm air tried to cool the engine. It was to be a severe test for the engine to get them to Basra.

The airspeed of their flight was now nearly 112 miles per hour (180 Km per hour) flat out and yet, hopping along following the winding bank Cobham wished at every mile that he might reach Basra by going faster still. However, the weather cleared into blue sky as the sand storm stopped and this gave Cobham the opportunity to climb to a more suitable height where he hoped for cooler air. At last, the great port of Basra came into view. The broad river was littered with shipping and the next problem was on knowing where to come down on the water? Basra was not on the original stopping list so no one expected their arrival and special moorings for their aircraft had not been arranged.

6: Urgent attention for Elliott

The landing on the river at Basra proceeded calmly except that upon taxiing into a landing stage the aircraft nearly hit deep-water marker buoys. It was difficult to manoeuvre to beach the aircraft as it bucked around in the fast flowing water, but he had to stop the engine to avoid overheating and if it had not been for an airman, a hospital patient named Brown, who jumped into the river fully clothed and steered 'FO' away from obstacles, the floats would have been crushed had the seaplane continued on the course it was taking.

Cobham looked through the cabin flap once more after cutting the engines to look at his friend. Elliott's head was still bowed and with the help of Brown he found Elliott to be seriously injured. Brown thought the injury looked serious, like a wound from an explosion! Together they each grabbed one of Elliott's arms and hoisted him out of the cabin, onto a float and with Brown in the water again, carried him over Brown's head onto the bank of the river.

Cobham explained to Brown that he had heard a noise above the sound of the engine and wondered what had happened and that they had to find a way to get him to hospital quickly as he had lost a lot of blood!

An official of The Anglo Persian Oil Company and an Inland Water Transport Officer got off a small boat and were promptly on the spot to administer some first aid. Local natives would not aid them having been frightened by the noise from the engine and the whirl of the propellers. The official raided a native house, because for an unexplained reason all house doors had been closed to them, and took out a mattress to use as a stretcher. Elliott was eventually moved in the base ambulance, which arrived some time later, to the Royal Air Force hospital where an operation was performed. But the surgeon and medical staff had taken some time to travel to where Cobham had landed and an unfortunate delay did not help Elliotts case. After several hours Cobham was informed that his friend was comfortable, although he did wonder if the delay might affect Elliott's progress because it had been some time since the damage to 'FO' had injured Elliott.

For the night 'FO' was towed down the river, closer to the RAF base, and then pushed between towering date palms in an irrigation canal to shelter it from any bad weather and the force of the tidal Shatt al-Arab river. The canal was about forty or fifty feet wide from bank to bank and the clear blue sky twinkled and struggled to penetrate through the bright green leaves. Under each palm tree was piled mounds of sand that had been dredged from the canal to prevent silting of the bottom. Regular attention was obviously necessary to maintain the flow.

During dinner that evening Cobham endeavoured to explain to the Commanding Officer how the accident had occurred but engineers present indicated that it was impossible for the petrol pipe to burst and do so much damage. The pipe was open ended and it was not a pressure pipe. It provided only for petrol to be lifted by using a manual operated pump, lifting the petrol to the top tank when necessary, from the spare petrol tank in the forward cabin.

Early the next morning an engineer officer informed Cobham that Arabs were present in the area over which they had flown and that it was indeed a bullet that had caused damage to "FO" and not the petrol pipe bursting. To prove this he took Cobham to the aircraft and showed him the route the bullet took.

The bullet had passed between the floats and then pieced the wall of the cabin. It had then gone through a despatch box, given by the Foreign Office to be delivered to the Governor-General of Australia, hit and punctured the fuel pipe and went on through Elliott's arm, into his side, then passed into his lung and ended buried under his right arm pit.

The next morning, "FO" was towed further down river and up

into the backwaters of the Royal Air Force inland water transport dock where it was moored for repairs caused by the bullet.

As he could not continue without Arthur Elliott and the aircraft was being repaired, Cobham therefore decided to make the journey to Nasiriyah, near the ancient city of Ur, to find the area where he thought someone, maybe an Arab, had fired at his aircraft. A Squadron Leader Stoddart accompanied him in the station aircraft, from the airfield at Shiba, a suburb of Basra, in an endeavour to locate the Tribe to which the person who shot at the plane belonged. The journey did not take long and after meeting with the Police at Nasiriyah they returned to hear bad news.

Whilst Cobham was away matters turned for the worst and Elliott had a massive heart attack and died. The loss of blood during the flight to Basra after the injury had taken its toll. Alan Cobham was inconsolable. Elliott had become a great and trusted friend.

The day began hot and a strong wind produced a haze of sand. Close to irrigation canals for a date palm farm, outside of the city centre is the Makinah cemetery where the war graves listing thousands of veterans of the 1914-18 Great War are buried. Prompt arrangements were made for the funeral of Arthur Elliott because the extreme temperature would have rendered a corpse unbearable in a few hours. Elliott died in the RAF hospital at 11.30 am on July 6th .The funeral took place at Sunset with RAF personnel lining the entrance and Group Captain CEH Rathbourne DSO being a representative of the A.O.C. forces in Iraq. Eight khaki clad airmen carried the coffin.

Cobham did not want to continue the flight. However, he was persuaded to consider continuing, as a tribute to his friend on condition that an engineer could be found at Basra. A replacement from England would take too long, because time was important to avoid the Monsoon's bad weather.

Group Captain Rathbourne commanding RAF Squadron 84 decided to approach one of his flight engineers Sergeant Arthur Ward and explained that Mr.Cobham's engineer had died in the base hospital and Mr. Cobham was looking for a replacement, otherwise he would call off the historic flight to Australia and back to England. They were looking for a volunteer to take Mr Elliot's place. He thought Ward might like to consider volunteering? If he were to say yes the matter would still have to be ratified by the Air Officer Commanding and maybe the owner of the aircraft. He asked Ward to think it over for a few hours and come and see him again the next morning.

Sergeant Arthur Ward RAF Aircraft Fitter, of the RAF 84 Squadron thanked the Group Captain and said he would give it some thought, but then added a question that he had heard a rumour that the engineer, Mr.Elliott, died because of a defective fuel pipe on the aircraft. Was the rumour true, he wanted to know?

The Group Captain explained that the presumption was a broken fuel pipe that caused the injuries to Elliott, but informed him that it was established beyond any doubt that he was shot. The bullet penetrated the fuselage, then glanced off the petrol pipe through Mr.Elliott's arm and into his chest. It resulted in a rib and arm being broken and the lung pieced. It was supposed that some up-country Arab seeing the aircraft flying low, took a shot at it, somewhere in the Khor-al-Hammer district of Nasiriyah 100 miles north of Basra.

Ward said he would like to know more and meet with Cobham and also have a close look at his aircraft.

However, the Group Captain said a meeting was not possible as Mr Cobham had just returned from Nasiriyah, close to where his engineer was shot. He and with Squadron Leader Stoddart had been trying to locate the tribe to which the Arab, who fired the shot, belonged. Mr Cobham was resting after a very taxing day having also attended the funeral of Mr.Elliott. The Group Captain suggested that Ward should visit the inland water dock where he was sure he would find Mr Cobham's seaplane. He passed a note that he asked should be given to the military policeman on duty guarding Mr Cobham's aircraft, allowing Ward access.

The Group Captain explained to Ward that Cobham's aircraft for the flight to Australia and back, G-EBFO, was a De Havilland DH50j bi-plane and Alan Cobham being the senior test pilot at De-Havilland had already won the 1924 King's Cup Air Race at an average speed of 107 mph in the prototype DH 50, G-EBFN using a 240hp Puma engine. Its successor "FO" for short had already flown to South Africa and back by Cobham with Elliott as his engineer using an Armstrong Siddeley Jaguar 385 horsepower rated engine.

Ward thanked his Group Captain, saluted and left his office.

Sergeant Arthur Ward was 25 years old and had joined the Royal Flying Corps (later to become the Royal Air Force or RAF as was also to be known) at the age of 16 years as an apprentice. He was the oldest of nine children from a poor family living near Kings Cross, London and it may have been a relief to his parents that he found employment with the RFC.

Ward had a little technical knowledge of the 385hp Jaguar engine whilst serving in the RAF in England. It was a modern radial air-cooled type and had not been used in the Middle East. If Cobham wanted an engineer to take Elliott's place then he was the only mechanic in Iraq to meet most of the requirements. The alternative would be to wait some three weeks for a replacement from England, which was unlikely, thought Ward.

When they met, Cobham asked Ward how much knowledge he knew about the Jaguar 385 engine?

Ward explained he worked on the Jaguar 385 engine for a short while in England. It suffered from vibration problems due to a lack of a crankshaft centre bearing. But it was a powerful engine he had been told, especially after the pistons were bored to increase in size. He did not have any manuals with him in Basra because they do not have the same make of engine in that country. He assumed Mr. Elliott had detailed manuals about the engine?

Cobham said that Ward would find them in the map pocket in the cabin. There was also a duplicate set in the flight bag, which was in Cobham's room. He asked Ward to let him talk the manuals through with him and then said Elliott had been an excellent engineer who supervised the installation of the Jaguar 385 engine when it was changed from the original Pantha 240. Ward could see that Cobham was very disturbed about the death of Elliott.

Whilst the engine was very important to Sergeant Ward he was also aware that the airframe, which supported the engine and the wings and the fuel tanks and of course the equipment, were just as important. In this respect Arthur Ward took his time in inspecting, as thoroughly as he could with the time span available, nearly every nut and bolt, strut of wire and canvas holding the aircraft together.

Then he checked the instruments; first the airspeed indicator that was a spring and flap and a resistant pad operated by an electric resister pushed back by the speed of the wind, the compass, then the fuel gauges, the altimeters, the rev counters, temperature gauge, the controls, steering column, ailerons and elevators and foot controls for the rudder. He checked the trim controls, the petrol on off controls and the damaged pipes from the fuel tank. His findings found 'FO' to be a sound aircraft. He was not aircrew but he made up his mind, he would go with Alan Cobham as his engineer, if asked to do so.

Sargent Ward, a brave and excited man, then asked when could they leave?

First, they had to gain permission from the Royal Air Force and also from the sponsor, Sir Charles Wakefield and also the owner of 'FO', the De Havilland Aircraft Company, to take him on the rest of the journey, explained Cobham. Meanwhile, he should get together his travel gear and any clothing of Elliotts that would fit. The airmen had specialised clothing which could be necessary to protect from the cold as they approached Melbourne from over the mountains. He should remember also that they have a weight problem to take into account and to weigh everything to calculate the total weight given that Ward needed extra items!

Cobham continued that the De Havilland DH50j was an aircraft designed to be a maximum 4500 pounds weight whereas, "FO" was about 5450 pounds, but despite the fact she was nearly 1000 pounds heavier, she was behaving very well. However, he had it in mind to change the propeller at some time when the different pitch of the blade would improve their lift off. He explained that the damaged pipes were being taken out and replaced by the RAF airframe fitters.

8: Leaving Basra

July 11th

The Times Newspaper reported that ' Mr Alan Cobham said tonight he had obtained permission from Air Vice Marshall Higgins to take an Air Force Mechanic for the continuation of the flight to Australia. He said, he will take Sergeant Ward, who was a charming young fellow and a Cockney like himself, and added that Sergeant Ward was unmarried, belonged to number 84 (Bombing) Squadron, Shaibah. He was a clever engineer and popular in the Squadron and had some experience of the Jaguar engine in England. To him one engine is like another and there is no need now to wait three weeks for anyone to come out from England. Cobham continued by saying he is leaving at dawn on Tuesday 13th July. Everything is now ready and they are only waiting for a message, from De Havilland, agreeing to his taking Ward, who is this morning servicing the engine.'

In the Officer Commanding's office farewell drinks were laid out on a table and behind this stood Group Captain Rathbourne, some Officers and Non Commissioned Officers of the airbase, who were also by the Group Captain's side, being attentive as Rathbourne wished Cobham and Ward a safe voyage.

He said it looked like they will be leaving shortly and on behalf of the men there, wished them every success with the remainder of the journey. Ward was a conscientious mechanic and he will do a good job for Mr Cobham. Incidentally, he heard the police have arrested a tribesman at Hamer Lake in connexion with the shooting of Elliott. If Mr Cobham was able, he asked him to please keep in touch!

Cobham thanked him, for his speech and for allowing Sergeant Ward to accompanying him and continue on the first long distance flight to Australia and back to England. He recalled that he was still suffering the loss of Elliott who had become a good friend. However, the future of long distance commercial flights would be indebted to the Group Captain, and he would do his best to look after Ward and hand him back in one piece.

July 13th

Once alongside the landing stage by the RAF dock area, final checks of the fuselage were made. Cobham tested the wing stays for approximate stress by twanging the stays, like playing a harp. The ailerons on the lower of the two wings, rudder and tail wings were inspected for any damage and the floats were inspected. Ward followed Cobham closely to confirm that all tests had been completed satisfactory and to understand the routine Cobham required.

Ward supervised the refuelling from a tank on the back of a lorry, pumped by hand. After refuelling Cobham conducted instrument tests, to establish that each one showed a dial reading when the electrical current was switched on. All of the tests and inspection routines were standard regulations before taking off and if faults were found either replacements would be made or a decision made to continue the flight with repairs being made at a later stage, should it be safe to do so. The test routine for long distance flying was more complicated but the aircraft had received an overhaul and intensive service by the RAF mechanics and engine fitters so only a visual inspection might be required at this time, except that the engine overhaul had to be supervised by Ward.

Eventually Ward loaded the holdalls of both his and Cobham's possessions into the cabin and placed his valuable tool bag behind the seat that was in front of him. It was an engineer's responsibility to have with him his own tool bag, at all times. Using someone else's tool bag was totally foreign to any engineer or tradesman. Elliott's tool bag was placed in the area behind Cobham's cockpit, just in case something extra might be of use during the flight, despite adding to the weight of 'FO' with both tool bags..

Cobham having lodged his flight plan with Air Traffic Control, which he would do at every departure point if there was a Controller, raised his hand towards a mechanic who prepared to empty the landing stage of personnel. The ignition switch was primed and Cobham started the engines using the internal battery that rotated the starter motor. This in turn rotated the propeller and the engine started into action at about 1150 revolutions per minute. At this low engine speed, it was still difficult to hold the aircraft close to the landing stage and therefore Cobham needed to quickly get out to the middle of the river.

Should the battery be flat at any time a winding starter handle, forward on the starboard side of the fuselage behind the engine manually started the engine, usually first time, but was not easy to operate. Cobham nearly always chose the starter handle method to maximise battery performance. However, this meant that the engineer had to balance carefully on the floats and getting back into the forward cabin, using the foot slots built into the side wall of the fuselage and against the airflow, was difficult.

As the engine was air-cooled, and the ambient temperature was high, it was important to take off quickly and therefore within four minutes Cobham dropped his hand to indicate they were ready to proceed into the main flow of the Tigris River. Airmen using poles with large pads on the end pushed the aircraft away from the landing stage. They nearly fell over from the airflow of the engine as Cobham opened up the throttle to keep the floats away from the wooden supports of the landing stage.

Cobham took the aircraft out towards the middle of the Tigris River and turned into the wind that was fairly calm. The wind always increased as the day heated up, unless a storm was brewing when it would be uncomfortable for long periods. The sand got into everything possible on land and on water the wind would churn the surface, mixing with the sand, and the propeller would accelerate spray into the face of the pilot, making it hard to see. Today it was fairly calm and the take-off from the water at about forty miles an hour was satisfactory. The heat during the later part of the morning made for thinner air making lifting an already overloaded aircraft, difficult.

It was 6am. The plane gained speed and Ward wondered whether it would ever take off, but quickly and without feeling they were about thirty feet in the air turning towards the coast of Persia and just clearing the Date Palms that stretched before them. The noise was horrific in the tiny cabin behind the engine and the ear pads of his helmet were of little help in reducing the roar, but as they climbed somehow Ward found the sound had been reduced by the airflow over the wings and around the airframe making the problem just about bearable. They were now leaving Iraq and the ancient Mesopotamia that saw the rise of the first civilization in World history, over five thousand years before, and for Cobham the bad memories of the death of Elliott.

9: Avoid Persia

Cobham had received a telegraph message from the British Embassy in Baghdad shortly before leaving Basra that the Persian Consul in Ahwaz had said they should not pass over Persian territory at the Ahwaz zone because of a terrorist uprising. This would involve going 70 miles out from the direct route. They therefore would have to stop at Bushire to refuel because the hot climate meant that 'FO' had to use more fuel to keep at a safe height in an extreme of air temperature.

The Ahwaz air space included the Khuzestan Province of Persia and Cobham elected to fly to Bubiyan Island at the southern tip of Persia before cutting along the coast and hopping among the Islands close to Bander-e Khomeyni.

They flew along the coast of the Gulf with blue sky above and a gentle haze below them. Ward studied the Flight Log that had details of the journey, for detailing the compass bearings, distance to be travelled, land marks of importance and hazards for each leg. Apart from the technical training he received as an apprentice he also studied navigation, more as a hobby than ever thinking he should be involved with actually becoming aircrew. Now his hobby was more than an interest; he could assist the pilot.

Ward wondered where the bullet had come into the aircraft, as he looked out of the side window. He tried to imagine the route it took and wondered if other damage occurred which had not been seen and could prove to be a problem later in the flight. Did they have on board sufficient spare parts, he now wondered? 'You can always take an extra aircraft for spares, Sergeant,' his Corporal had chided before they left Basra.

Cobham, in his isolated cockpit was forever looking at instruments or out of the cockpit analysing the sky ahead. He suddenly

46

noticed that petrol in the top tank was getting low. Normally they carried at least fifty gallons of petrol in the top tank, which fed the engine carburettors by gravity feed. A separate tank inside the cabin contained a further hundred gallons with which the flight engineer topped up the top tank by using a manual pump when necessary.

To save weight Cobham had dispensed with a windmill style automatic petrol pump used in normal circumstances.. The engineer in the cabin could easily feed the top tank when instructed to do so by the pilot.

On this occasion, when instructed to pump manually, because the gauge showed half empty, Ward commenced to pump with maximum energy, but after ten minutes no progress was evident and Cobham yelled through to Ward telling him to pump harder because something was wrong.

With no fuel reaching the top tank Cobham doubted whether he could reach Bushire on the remaining fuel. Ward, by this time, was getting exhausted and if the hand pump were not already broken it would be very soon.

Cobham then remembered that there was a petrol turnoff tap at the top of the pump which Ward may not have known about, and it must have been turned off whilst the aircraft was being serviced. He shouted to Ward, through the cabin tube, that there was a petrol cock turnoff at the base of the pump and to turn it on!

Ward found the valve and turned it on. The petrol gauge started to rise as the pump was primed and their worries were over.

The terrain under them was white sand on the port side and aquamarine sea on the starboard side. 'FO' passed over isolated fishing boats that were making their way to Bushire with their catch. Bushire (Also known as Bushehr) was once the terminus of an important caravan route servicing the Ottoman Empire. It subsequently became an important British Naval base and was prominent as the British diplomatic and commercial headquarters for the Persian Gulf. It was also an important fishing town.

Ward entered in the aircraft travel log with the following : Date

13th July 1926 Basra to Bushire, depart 06.10, arrived Bushire 08.50, total time flown 2.40 hours.

'FO' made a descent into the waters of the port weaving through fishing boats of many shapes and sizes that sported sails of many colours. Cobham landed the aircraft, when at about 40 miles per hour he cut back the throttle, and with a few jumps on the way touched the water then turned towards the fuel jetty that was bedecked in flags of many Nations. Cobham docked the aircraft close to the jetty and handed the re-fuelling to Ward. They had been flying for about three hours and Ward, not yet used to being cramped in a small cabin was grateful for the interlude. He could sit up but could not walk around. There was one other seat in front on this aircraft where normally there would be three seats. However storage space was needed, also a reduction in weight so one seat had been taken out.

Shortly before re-fuelling was complete Cobham returned to inform Ward that they would be staying for a while and would be leaving when it was cooler, some time in the early evening. They would have sufficient daylight, he calculated, to make their scheduled stop if they left shortly after six.

This lull in the schedule gave Ward the opportunity to check the oil filter, which might give an indication of any internal problems with the engine and also ensure that no grit or foreign matter was to be seen that could harm the engine and affect the oil pressure.

After every flight, petrol filters were always cleaned and the valve springs and valve stems inspected. A general system of overhaul, maintenance and inspection was always put into practice.

After refuelling and checking the engine, Cobham and Ward left Bushire at 6.40pm in order to arrive at Bandar-e-'Abbas by 9.30pm, certainly before the heat of the day.

10: A difficult mooring

The land formation took on wonderful colouration as the aircraft proceeded down the Persian Gulf. The vivid colours and mountains of varying hues astounded Ward as he looked out from his cabin through one of four small windows on the side at head height. More small windows were situated on the top of the fuselage that was hinged so that the occupants of the cabin could get out. But the top wing restricted the view and only became useful during banking of the aircraft. The area in front of him to the port side ran a mosaic of gems ranging from green to turquoise to bright blue with yellow hills and bright red rocks divided by the silver streaks of dried up river beds.

As they arrived at their next stop Cobham was dismayed to find that a strong sea was flowing and a wind was blowing across the waves so that landing was going to be difficult. Pilots expect to land into wind; landing across the waves might force one of the floats under the sea and tip the aircraft over.

Cobham decided to forget the wind factor that could reduce their landing speed to about twenty miles an hour, and instead landed head on to the waves. Because of the long interlude between waves they landed safely.

The moment they landed "FO" was buffeted by the waves, but a motor launch came out to meet them and Ward left the cabin to throw to the crew of the launch, a rope, to tow the aircraft to the shore where the it was beached. Ward stayed with the aircraft and Cobham got transport across the wet sand, with four natives giving him a chair lift.

The area used for seaplane and small boats was to the south east of the busy commercial Port of Bander-e-Abbas. The area, as far as the eye could see, was a flat terrain with an altitude of about thirty feet (9 meters). The average daily temperature is 103 deg. (39 deg.C) hot and humid. The port supported fishing with a population in 1926 of an estimated 12,000 people. The soil is sand and Banda-e-Abbas was in Persia.

In 1935 the country was changed Internationally to Iran, by the Reza Shah, the ruler at that time asking the World to recognise the Country as Iran, although historically it was always known as Iran by the population for many centuries when they discovered they were an Aryan race of people who were supposed to be the best race. When Aryan is translated into Arabic it becomes Iran. It was a mistake made by the educated Greeks who called it Persia. Winston Churchill, the British Prime Minister during the Second World Ward referred to it as being Persia in Cabinet papers because it was a very similar name to Iraq that had British influence and Iran had German influence. (See 'Why did Persia change its name to Iran', in the Public domain). But in 1926 the country was still known internationally as Persia.

After going ashore Cobham met up with a friend, Doctor Mackay who was to receive them, under an awning with cold drinks and lots of ice. A ship had arrived that day and had left a supply. Ice applied to Cobham's neck revived him after the hot humid flight.

Cobham was informed that a storm was brewing and 'FO' must be moored further out to sea because there had been forecast an extraordinary low tide and 'FO' could be bounced around on the seabed. Alternatively a low tide also could mean that should the wind drive the waves ashore "FO" could be lifted by the waves and dropped onto the floats with perhaps a disastrous effect.

It was decided, therefore that Cobham and Ward would get up at one o'clock in the morning and hold the machine down until the sea was under it, then tow her out to a safe depth. After an hour and a half they could re-beach the machine safely.

A local bank manager awakened them at 1am in the morning and they were given tea on the veranda of the hotel. Cobham was so exhausted after his journey that it took all his will power to avoid drifting back asleep.

By the light of an old oil lamp, because the night was pitch black without a moon, they set out with a guide over sand dunes to reach the aircraft on the beach. Six natives, in a rowing boat, were waiting to help float "FO" out to a mooring. Within ten minutes the tide had brought in the sea and the aircraft began to float and was pulled out to sea.

The monsoon was beginning to be a problem but there was no turning back. However, there are no rocks and plenty of open sea at Bander Abbas and no obstructions except a motor launch called the "Felix Jones" which belonged to the British Consul. At the time it was moored out in the sea, about four hundred yards from "FO" and could just be seen as a dim outline as their eyes became used to the darkness.

Ward warned the natives to be aware of the launch but they seemed not to understand, and in fact had lost sight of the buoy and were intending to tie the seaplane to the "Felix Jones" as a substitute. There was no interpreter aboard the rowing boat so Cobham decided that, whilst not ideal, both seaplane and launch would swing more or less into the wind and "FO" would be perfectly safe until the morning. However, there was a strong current running at the time and the desirable approach to the launch was against the current, but the natives towed the seaplane around the bow of the launch so that "FO" drifted onto it.

With so much sea and only one obstruction the moment the natives stopped rowing to fasten a line the seaplane drifted with the current and naturally an accident was bound to happen because the tow line was long and ceased to be of any use for towing as "FO" drifted into the launch.

When the crash happened to Cobham's precious aircraft, which had brought him all the way from England, it had collided with the rails of the launch and they could hear the cracking of timbers and the fragile wings breaking as the waves moved the aircraft towards the launch. Ward jumped down on to the front of the starboard float to push the seaplane away and Cobham moved to the rear of the float to prevent the tail being damaged as the aircraft turned into the launch. However, by this time the damage looked serious and would require attention.

Cobham shouted at the natives to assist by coming out of the rowing boat and to get on-board the launch to keep the seaplane away from the launch handrails. He decided that "FO" should be towed back to the beach.

The natives by now knew they would lose face should they were to tow the aircraft back to the beach and they were reluctant to obey the new instruction. However, with threats of 'Physical harming or even death' or words to that effect, the natives eventually towed the seaplane to the beach where it was pulled up as high as possible away from the water to await the morning light. A guard was set up and Cobham and Ward retired to their bedrooms exhausted beyond belief.

11: Damage to FO

Their rooms were typical of the Middle East. Each was dark and illuminated by candles carefully placed on walls. The bathroom attached to each was situated on part of the terrace, but secluded with the odd missing brick placed to allow air to flow through into the bedroom; a common design to cool buildings used throughout the Middle East.

The next morning an inspection of the wing tips and the tail showed that the damage was not nearly as bad as they thought and they were able to have the aircraft ready for a midday take-off with a few minor repairs and lots of fish glue.

Refuelling had to be carried out by hand by Ward, with assistance from the fuel supplier, from a flat bottom boat. Because of the high tide and high breakers at the shore edge they decided once more to move the aircraft to a deeper mooring. It was extremely difficult to manhandle the fuel cans from the boat, which rocked side to side, and up onto the top of the tank which was positioned above the top wing. Refuelling the cabin fuel tank was easier but still required a lot of care and concentration considering the buffeting given to 'FO' by the sea.

Refuelling took some time and Ward was very grateful when it was completed. He climbed aboard and slid into his seat in the forward cabin. The seat was more a pile up of gear for the journey that Ward had moulded around the basic seat frame into a comfortable resting place and waited for Alan Cobham to arrive. The heat of the day was getting at him and he felt sleepy.

By this time the sea was rough again but the breakers were quite moderate and some fishermen assured Cobham that out at sea the waves would not do serious harm, so they warmed up the engine.

Their speed increased but because 'FO' was overweight it was going to take a long time before it lifted off the water. At each wave crest the sea hit the floats with a heavy thud. Should the distance between the wave crests change, the floats could dive down below the next wave crest, reduce the speed and tip the aircraft forward and the water could hit the propeller and get into the engine or the fuselage.

It was no easy matter to control the aircraft and as he came over a crest he saw to his horror that the waves in front were too high. In a second he pulled back the throttle and waited and prayed in the pitching sea that they would not be swamped, and damage be done to 'FO'.

As the engine slowed the aircraft sank deeper into the sea with the waves causing sickening thuds. At last they stopped and a new difficulty occurred because it was vital to keep 'FO' into the wind. Should the aircraft turn broadside to a wave the wingtips might be thrust under a wave and the wing broken.

Luckily, it drifted backwards with the wind until it was deep and calm enough for the natives to wade or swim out to it. But the natives then tried to turn 'FO' around so that she could be hauled up the beach, but frontwards. Ward climbed out onto the floats and with using his toe and much shouting he gently prodded any native who desired to turn the aircraft and in this way they came to the beach facing the waves.

Once on the beach they found that a wing strut had been broken, which necessitated a further delay for repairs. Ward set about taking the damaged strut off and with the help of a local garage was able to make an expert repair. He replaced the strut within two hours. He also found spare parts for another aircraft at an aircraft store and these made for a perfect fit, after a blacksmith had made the round tube into an oval and Ward had pushed the spare part inside the repaired strut to provide extra strength.

The weather deteriorated and no more could be done to hasten a departure except to repeat the process of the night before and move "FO" out at high tide and bring her back again as the tide receded, twice each day.

In the evening Alan Cobham retired to bed but Ward decided to get some exercise and went out to walk a few blocks to sample some of the nightlife. He found a bar with entertainment in the form of a 'Belly Dancer'. She was a big woman, but never the less knew how to wobble the huge amount of flesh that surrounded her waist. He ordered a scotch 'On the rocks' which turned out to be a glass of ice and a small bottle containing an insipid looking liquid with a cap that had already been opened. The bottle had at some time held alcohol because there was a label confirming this fact, but Ward decided not to chance the drink and walked out leaving the bottle on the table. He went back to the hotel and was soon asleep.

12: A thermal current

Bandar-e-'Abbas is situated opposite the Musandam Peninsula at the northern tip of Oman. It is where the Persian Gulf and the Gulf of Oman, or also known as the Arabian Sea, meet. Strange tidal conditions occur which can affect wind patterns.

As the hour of departure approached on the 18th July the weather became cloudy and the sea developed a heavy swell. Ward could see several large ships making their way to the shelter of the docking area of the Port. 'This was not a day to be travelling by air', he was thinking!

However, Cobham had already signed for fuel at an office near the landing stage. He alighted from a launch and bade farewell to his host and also to the driver of the launch, which was by now banging against the starboard float. He shouted to the driver to be careful as he pointed down to the floats.

Ward had to agree that any damage done to any of the floats might severely delay their progress. An experienced workshop would be needed to repair more serious damage and although local aircraft would be seaplanes and have repair facilities somewhere along the coast, any delay in getting repairs done would seriously impede the flight plans.

Ward's responsibility on departure was to climb out onto the starboard float, and at Cobham's command, proceeded to turn the handle that turned the crankshaft of the engine. The engine started immediately and the turning handle disengaged easily to avoid any damage to the operator. Then he held onto the float strut and edged forward until he was able to pull on the rope that passed from the aircraft to the buoy and back. Those aboard the launch, who stood by in case of a problem, such as 'Man overboard' observed that this was not easy to do against the airflow of the propeller.

Ward pulled in the part of the rope connected to the aircraft, which slipped through the ring of the buoy. He untied the knot and coiled the rope ready to be taken on board. 'FO' drifted backwards by the force of the wind as Ward edged carefully towards his cabin and climbed in. He was nearly dislodged by the airflow from the engine, that Cobham had increased in revolutions to maintain position in the wind and current and avoid any possible damage. He struggled with the cabin hatch but made the sanctuary of his seat.

Storms battered the Bandar-e-Abbas area but, Cobham decided to chance the journey to Chabaha and they left at an early hour, about six am taking off in a choppy sea. It was a difficult journey. The storm was mainly pushing them from behind but the rain was being pulled through the propeller and Cobham found it very difficult to see ahead of them. Ward put up with a very bumpy flight and was thrown about, feeling very uncomfortable. He would have to get used to the conditions if he was to survive the journey.

After a few hours of difficult flying they descended and landed on the sea at Chabahar on the south side of Persia (Iran) where they refuelled from a native craft without putting a foot on shore.

The port is close by the City of Chabaha. It had not a long history and it was not until much later that it was developed into an important and much used seaport. The deep ocean around the port allowed for easy berthing of oversized vessels and cost of construction as a port benefitted from the depth. There was a fishing village called Tiz or later it was called Tis but was destroyed by the Mongols. The Sarhad mountain range, which runs north to south separates the sub continent of India from the Plateau of Persia.

Tis, eventually became Chabaha and was administered by India, but later became a major port of Iran, administered by Iran but with a free trading pact with India for continuing trade with Afghanistan.

They departed an hour later for Karachi in India. (Kaarachi is now the main port for Pakistan). Their planned route followed the coast of Baluchistan but the weather deteriorated further and Cobham was taken off course, and Cobham shouted through the voice tube asking Ward to look at his maps and try to determine where they were.

Ward replied, he could not see any water and that he sensed they were heading inland! He said that it appeared misty green below and perhaps they were heading for a mountain range north of Ormer Island. His recommendation was to turn south. Whether Cobham could hear all Ward had said did not matter because suddenly, a thermal current that sent them upwards hit 'FO'. Cobham pulled on the steering column and 'FO' turned backwards away from a rock face of the mountain that was shrouded in cloud.

Cobham eventually took control of his senses and headed in a southerly direction. The wind and rain seemed to cut into every part of his flying suit.

The first sighting of anything that could give them a bearing came shortly after when they both spotted, in a break in the clouds, the ravine leading from the shore to Rudeni Band on the Makran Coast, Pakistan. Cobham shouted that everything appeared alright and they were back on track. However, visibility was so bad that their eyes strained to see. Cobham assumed the next sighting should be a river inlet shortly after arable land that was irrigated by the river. He had no idea what the river's name was for his map did not list it and at this point he did not care either. The weather eased a little as 'FO' passed over a desert valley where water was plentiful and farmers grew wheat, cotton, rice, some vegetables and sugar cane. There were small cargo boats moored to a long jetty with men loading foodstuff and looked up to see 'FO' passing overhead.

They continued along the coast and Ward took out a small atlas to read about the Arabian Sea, above which they were flying. It is nearly three miles deep in parts. He looked over the side to gaze at the surface of the water that was black, and mumbled, that if they fell in would never be found!

They were now flying close to fertile plains and as they approached the Sonmiani Bay the weather became bad. The cloud cover fell to almost sea level but with the aid of the compass and altimeter

Cobham was able to steer towards Karachi, but he miscalculated the distance and they passed over Karachi without knowing it.

But suddenly, Ward shouted into the tube that he had sighted the harbour, on the port side!

Cobham had already seen the harbour and took 'FO' into a steep dive before turning into the safety of the harbour area where, having calculated his speed of approach he landed safely between flotillas of ships. It was the late afternoon and the dock area was very busy. They were pleased to have landed, but could not see a welcome party.

Karachi was the most important seaport of the Indian continent and became the grain exporting port of the British Empire. In 1926 an aerodrome was completed and became the airport for entry for the British Raj in India. But in 1926, India was emotionally tied in the belief that airships were the future and started to install a mast for securing airships to it. Being part of the Airship Communication scheme, the mast was later abandoned. So mixed were the views that debates ensued in many countries, stirred up by the Press, as to what constituted long distant travel. That was the reason for Cobham's flight to Melbourne and back to London, to prove that long distance flights with aircraft were commercially possible but with seaplanes insisted Cobham at that time.

13: The first monsoon

Their arrival in Karachi was totally unexpected owing to a previous report that their undercarriage had been damaged. The authority had not been informed the aircraft was a seaplane. However, after about ten minutes a launch arrived and Cobham and Ward were met by the Officer Commanding RAF Depot Karachi, who was a seaplane pilot. They heard later that the officer was looked upon, by his contemporaries, as being an expert and an authority on the subject of Cobham's landing.

Cobham cut the engine rather than let it get too hot and waited for the launch with the Office Commanding to take them in tow. Ward was standing on one float and Cobham on the other waiting for a mooring rope to be thrown so that one of them might catch it. But the first effort of throwing missed both of them. The Air Force man prepared to throw again. He took some time to recoil the rope and "FO" started to drift in the direction of some barges. Again the thrower cast the rope but it caught around a handrail on the launch. Then a third attempt he cast the rope but it got caught around his neck just as Cobham shouted that they were drifting towards the barges.

The shouts of both Cobham and Ward were wasted for there was no sign of the rope coming over to them and the barges were getting closer with every moment. The air was rife with adjectives as they both yelled but still the rope went through the slow process of being recoiled, untangled and made ready to throw. At last with a mighty effort, the thrower cast the rope and Ward managed to grab it as it floated on the water just within reach. On the launch there were many smiles and later Cobham found out that these were due to the fact that the heaver of the ropes was none other than the Officer Commanding himself.

It was with great relief that the two men found they were back in civilisation as they lay back in their host's car en route from the quayside to his house, where hot baths and clean clothing awaited them. The Royal Air Force had a service base in Karachi, which took over control of "FO" for the night and they overhauled and repaired any damage done at Banda Abbas. The floats were checked over and repainted, after the aircraft had been successfully towed out of the water on metal skids.

Both airmen were entertained in the Officers dining rooms that evening. In an after-dinner speech Cobham said he was glad to seize the opportunity of a temporary lull in the monsoon to get away from Bander Abbas where mountainous waves and hurricane-like winds caused him, and his engineer Ward, much anxiety as there was no shelter for the aircraft.

Later that night a cable was received at the dining table that read 'that sand-storms and rain were probable in the Rajpatana region by noon.'

He handed the report to Ward, sitting by his side, who asked, where Rajpatana was? Cobham explained it was in the north to central area of the Indian continent. He intended to follow the River Indis to Bahawalpur and stop there, after which proceed to Delhi. The journey across India, following carefully rivers and lakes would be a matter of dodging the monsoon at every turn, which precluded adherence to a fixed program. Whenever favourable they would push on to the next stopping place!

14: Mohamed

July 20th

They took off the next morning and headed northeast over the desert with a tail wind, but into a dust storm, that soon cleared. After about eighty miles they came to the River Indis and followed it until they arrived in Bahawalpur and landed on a tributary called the Sutlej River. At one point Cobham thought that he had mistaken one tributary for another but the great railway bridge before Bahawalpur came into view and he knew that they were on course. The landing was without problems except that the glare from the sun on the water was terrific and, despite wearing dark glasses, Cobham was troubled and in a gasping condition. It was with great relief, therefore, that the launch that towed them to the shore had a supply of ice to cool them. The temperature was 110 Fahrenheit (43 Centigrade) in the shade.

The police who arranged security for the aircraft and quarters for the night, met them. Cobham departed whilst Ward arranged for 'FO' to be refuelled and carried out an inspection of the floats, which had survived the landing.

The fuel tender eventually arrived at the quay. When the fuel was loaded Ward duly signed for it. By then the area around the aircraft was crowded with onlookers dressed in a variety of colourful clothing. The local crafts turned out a multitude of silk and cotton textiles.

Someone shouted from behind the throng of onlookers for Mr Arthur to follow him to take him to Mr Cobham. Ward could not see who was calling him. However, one of the policemen on duty guarding 'FO' raised his batten and threatened the crowd to arrange a safe passage to Ward's guide, who happened to be a small man who could not be seen above the crowd.

He announced his name as being Mohamed who wished to take him to the office of the Police authority where he will meet with Mr Cobham and pointed to his taxi that was standing in a side street. The vehicle was headed by a craggy small horse and attached was a four wheeled cart designed to carry passengers. It had a hood and was well equipped to carry two. The driver sat on a raised seat at the front and held the reigns and a small whip.

After Ward climbed aboard the driver pulled out into the crowd, which dispersed as he drove through them. They passed small dusty shops including a bakery where the finished hot bread was laid out on racks in the street. Next was a greengrocer selling a range of courgette, red, orange and green peppers and piled high, green melons.. The colours jumped out from the dusty background.

They came across a market area swarming with traders and other customers. Jewellery, trinkets and precious stones composed a whole section of stalls with stallholders leaning over magnifying glasses to evaluate a price.

Next they came upon a Mosque that towered above the area. A religious service was just starting with the call being made by a Mullah standing high in a Minaret on the side of the Mosque. Looking back Ward could see the stallholders quickly collecting together their valuables as the sounds of chanting began and all work stopped for prayers. The shutters quickly came down around any shop.

The driver pulled up close to a street merchant who sat there in his flowing robes, surrounded by bags of ground spices that he was busy closing to protect them, while he prepared to pray. The driver informed Ward, that he had to pray and would be back in about ten minutes. He asked that the horse be given some hay from a bag hanging down from the cart! The driver jumped off the cart and walked to the entrance of the Mosque.

By now there was a steady stream of worshipers moving towards the doors of the mosque and the area became quiet and strangely calm. The chanting from the Mullah ceased. All around shutters had been drawn over the shops and covers had been placed over the market stalls. It was slightly longer than ten minutes when Mohamed the driver returned to continue the journey that was easier now as the roads were reasonably clear as the Mosque cleared of worshipers. Eventually the taxi stopped at an official looking building and the driver announced it was the central police station.

Ward enquired if the driver had already been paid by Cobham and was told that he had. Mohamed lifted the bags off the cart for Ward to take in. After a dull evening, being entertained by the Commissioner of Police at the local hotel, both airmen retired to bed ready for an early start next morning.

15: Crossing India

July 21st. A crowded quay of local people waved in a gentle manner and saw the departure of Cobham and Ward from Bahawalpur at 6am. The air from the propellers blew clothing in all directions in such a way that it must have been difficult for those on the quay to see them.

Landing and take off on rivers is no easy matter, especially if there is a strong current running. At Bahawalpur it was not difficult because it was possible for the natives to stand in the water and hold the aircraft in position whilst the engine was started and warmed up. The conditions for take off were almost ideal as heading into the wind was also down current. Cobham had to be careful of a sand bank a little way down the river that he saw from the air prior to landing on the water.

Cobham had arranged with an interpreter that when he raised his hands above his head all of the natives should let go of the floats and he should open up the throttle to speed the engine and the aircraft would take off. With everything ready, and with Ward in the cabin, Cobham in his cockpit raised his hands above his head, and seeing the natives jump off, began to speed the aircraft along the water.

The art of taking off on water is to first prevent the floats from dipping into the water by pulling back on the joystick so that the elevators lift the nose of the aircraft. This operation is the opposite of taking off on land when the joystick is pushed forward to lift the tail before pulling back slightly to raise the aircraft into the air.

Cobham had just about reached the stage of lift off when he glanced sideways and saw that a native was still hanging on. It was only by sheer luck that Cobham looked that way, but the sandbank was coming upon him and he had to take off. He shouted at Ward who had seen what was happening and had already opened the flap of his cabin and very carefully started to climb out onto the wing. The airflow from the engine made it difficult, but he used his foot to stamp on the native's fingers whilst hanging on to a wing strut. With a howl the man slipped off the seaplane and fell into the river.

Ward's eyes followed the man down and he noticed that after hitting the water the man plunged deep below the surface. He got into the cabin, then shouted through the tube that he thought the man had gone under and they should fly around to make sure he was safe! Cobham, was already allowing the aircraft to slip sideways to make the turn at about a hundred feet in the air.

They both looked down and were pleased to see that a small boat had been used to pull the native from the water. They later learned that he was not a swimmer and could easily have drowned.

Looking back Ward could see the crowd on the quay disappear as they gained height and continued on their journey. Whilst the local population obtained their income mainly from farming, and servicing of farming equipment, factories producing engineering and textile products were expanding at a fast rate. Ward could see that several newly built buildings probably housed those activities.

The journey to Delhi followed a multitude of Irrigation Rivers that span the flat fertile Rajasthan and Punjab Plains. Cobham aimed for the town of Sirsa and then turned towards the Yamuna River, which guided him towards Delhi.

16: Delhi

They arrived in Delhi at about 11am and passed over the Red Fort, which once served as the Imperial Palace. It spread out below them for about one and a half miles and Cobham had to fly over the Fort at over three hundred feet to clear the top. Ward could observe re-construction work being carried out to many parts of the Fort, and there were waving hands from builders who worked upon flimsy scaffolding, constructed of bamboo tied with rope.

As they flew over the Delhi gate, one of the two massive gates by which the Fort is entered, they could see many people looking up at them. Looking down, Ward could see several pavilions, including the Khas Mahal, or Emperor's quarters, and formal gardens with many fountains making ingenious use of water. The whole area seemed to be made of red sandstone, including the walls, although they could also see shining white palaces situated inside. Wide roads separated the land around the beautiful houses and pavilions. The Red Fort is situated on the bank of the Yamuna River in Old Delhi, that is part of the city of Delhi, and was completed in 1648 for the Mughal King Shah Jahan. Alan Cobham related over their crude intercom tube that the Fort was over three hundred years old.

Cobham turned west away from the river and swept over Old Delhi, flying over the Jami Masjid, or old Mosque, built on an elevated site dating from 1650 to 1656, before turning back to the river where they landed close to a small island in sight of the Red Fort. The landing was difficult because the engine had started to misfire.

He kept the engine ticking over so as to get from the middle of the river to the safety of the shore where 'FO' arrived at a mooring. Ward got out onto one of the aircraft floats and with the boat hook managed to pull a mooring buoy to him and made fast the mooring rope. Then the engine suddenly stopped. Cobham tried to start the engine again by using the electric magneto starter but it refused to operate. The engine should have re-started easily. Ward then used the crank handle, all to no avail, except for a few turns of the propeller, some spluttering and a final stop.

An army officer welcomed them and issued an invitation to dine at the officers club. Cobham replied that he was very thankful of the invitation but would it be possible to confirm later when they had inspected the engine, which was causing a few problems? He turned to Ward and enquired what could be the problem?

17: Repairs to 'FO'

Ward decided to start to find the non-starting problem, by changing the spark plugs, but it was getting too dark and in any case the engine was too hot. And so he arranged to refuel that evening, instead, and put in for an early call the next morning to attend to the engine.

Cobham mentioned to Ward that they should leave later in the morning for Allahabad. He would cable ahead from the Army signals section to say it will not be tonight. They would upset the crowd of supporters who had been waiting several hours for their arrival but they could not help that. He recommended a wash and brush up and after that they would meet in the officer's dining room, say eight o'clock. He was informed that he would find the quarters to be past the street market in Old Delhi, which he could not miss!

Ward was by now very tired and although he agreed to a meeting with Cobham he would willingly have settled for an early night. He waited for the fuel tender to arrive and in twenty minutes the hand pumps had filled the top and cabin tanks and all that was required was to wait for the security guards, supplied by the army, to arrive. He then left to find quarters that had hurriedly been prepared for him because this was an unscheduled stop.

He found himself to be passing through Old Delhi and was struck by the variety of the view. The street scene was hectic, reflecting the traditional role the town offered as a meeting place for Muslim and Hindu cultures.

He passed rows and rows of rickshaw and carriages waiting for customers. Spice stalls were everywhere and little shops hid behind ornate, hand crafted shop signs. The area buzzed with traders and Ward trod carefully between the hoards of merchandise until, eventually, he arrived at a guarded entrance to the army barracks.

Ward approached the Military Policeman at the barrier, and announced his name and said he was to be billeted in the building but before he completed his sentence he was ushered through the barrier in the direction of a hut inside the barracks where he found a Corporal, who asked another soldier to take Ward to his sleeping quarters.

It was now about six in the evening. Ward was very tired so he asked the soldier to arrange a wake up call for him at seven thirty so as to meet with Cobham at eight pm. He took off his shoes and sank into the straw filled mattress falling asleep almost immediately.

The next morning Ward pulled out bags full of spares from an underside hatch of the aircraft and laid out some tools and spare parts for the engine, watched by a crowd of onlookers. He laid a canvas sheet under the nose and stretched the canvas over two poles extended forward of the engine. This was to catch anything dropped whilst servicing the engine because being moored out in the water away from the bank, anything dropped overboard would not be found again..

Chaos during refuelling.

He used a plug spanner to undo the topside engine spark plug, which seemed to be dry and nearly clean. The radial engine had other plugs positioned around a three hundred and sixty degree circumference. Each was taken out and inspected and were found to be in good order.

He next traced the cable from each spark plug back to the distributor and tested each circuit. Again, all was in order and so he checked the fuel lines and the carburettor. There were no problems as far as he could see.

Cobham recommended trying to start the engine again, but whilst the engine turned over and spluttered, as before, it would not start.

It was then that Cobham remembered that at each stop it was his practice to wedge a large piece of rag in the air-intake pipe to prevent sand getting into the carburettor. Two of these pieces of rag had been sucked way down into the pipes and when, with difficulty, they were removed the engine started first time.

It was on this occasion that Ward made a note in his log that the problem was not caused by any mistake made by himself. He was naturally upset that the incident could have been fatal to the journey and themselves!

July 22nd. Cobham and Ward left Delhi in the morning at 10am but not without problems. A seaplane moored on water is like a weathercock on a roof and always when moored will, like a boat, head into the wind. In this case as the current was pushing into the shore, the aircraft was facing into the wind towards the far bank, and in this situation Cobham was going to find it difficult to lift off.

Ropes were fixed from both banks so that "FO" could be turned to face along the river and the mooring rope was cast off. However, one of the holding ropes broke and suddenly the aircraft was in danger of crashing against a stone embankment. Ward, wearing only a bathing costume, jumped into the river and held on to the float to prevent an accident.

At this point a plucky native army sergeant major came forward and volunteered to solve the problem. He and Ward would push the aircraft out and as long as they could touch the river bottom they would have control additional to ropes, which were now held by police from each side of the bank. Ward was then to get into the cabin and the sergeant major would get onto the float close to where all the ropes were fed between the float stays. Cobham was then to open up the engine and start the journey along the river.

The Police, on each side holding the ropes, would have to run along the bank until the sergeant major saw Cobham waving his arms to tell them to release the ropes then he would jump off into the river. He was a good swimmer, he confided to Cobham who had no reason to doubt him. It was to be the second time a man would be cast off his ascending seaplane. Life was not boring, he later recalled.

The ropes were several hundred feet long, doubled on either side, and so there was sufficient rope to be let out to get up speed. Cobham headed out and quickly got up to thirty miles an hour and raised his arm. The sergeant instantly set to work feeding the ropes through the float stays and when the last rope had been released and the aircraft by now was travelling at forty miles per hour and lifting off the water, the sergeant major gently slid off the float and hit the water hard and disappeared out of sight. As they flew back over the river they were pleased to see that he had got to the shore and was waving them goodbye.

They arrived at Allahabad flying low over the Yamura River until it joined with the Ganges River. Allahabad is one of three most important religious centres in India. The River flows from caves over three thousand metres above sea level in northern India and 1560 miles further on, flows into the Bay of Bengal, south of Calcutta.

Whilst flying to Allahabad Ward saw a large tiger close to the waters edge of the Yamura River, one of the most polluted rivers in the world, and not far from Allahabad. He shouted down into the tube and through the hatch pointed it out to Cobham, who dived to get a better view, but the noise of the engine frightened the tiger that ran for the cover of the bush. It was a magnificent beast and looked to be fully mature.

There was a crowd to meet them as they touched down into turbulent waters, but after a few bounces, Cobham placed the aircraft in the ideal direction against the flow of the water and the wind. They taxied to a mooring between large tanks that had been put in place to mark the landing area. They were very large and required some skill to steer between. Cobham managed to do this with only a slight bump and damage to one float. Ward got onto the float and soon tied up to the mooring buoy.

Cobham looked out and was disturbed to see several native boats put out from the shore to get a better look at them. Every native boatman who had a craft was to make money that day, having crammed in more than the maximum number of passengers until each boat was in danger of collapsing and tossing out it's cargo. The boatmen endeavoured to row around the aircraft and as there was a strong current running they only narrowly missed doing damage to the wings by steering to left or right at the last moment.

The next problem involved the barge that the Burma Oil Company lowered from the banks of the river on strong ropes with all of their fuel on and semi-rotary pumps for speed filling. To see this ugly, heavily laden craft with barrels of BOC fuel float precariously close to "FO" held off by several natives taking hold of the wing and tail wing in a fast six knot current, with other boats cruising too close for comfort, brought tears to Cobham's eyes.

It was then that, shouting, he demanded the 'bloody idiots' should be careful of the floats and wings and must get away from the aircraft and be 'bloody' careful! Ward could do no more than look, pray or close his eyes, but within twenty minutes loading the fuel was completed and a police boat came out to drop security personnel for the night and the sightseeing boats departed.

18: The Tiger

They stayed the night at the ancient fort situated at the point where the Jumuna and the Ganges rivers meet. It is rarely open to the public but there are few rooms that can be used for an overnight stay by visiting personnel associated with the military. The fort grounds include the ten-meter high Ashok Pillar said to have been built in the year 232 BC. The sand banks alongside the fort make it suitable for the annual Hindu religious ritual of bathing, especially on steps leading down from the banks of the River Ganges which flowed along the east side of the city. Allahabad is one of the holiest and oldest cities in India, visited by thousands of Hindu pilgrims, each year.

They each had a room with walls built ten to twenty feet thick and being enormous in size. Cobham looked out from the balcony that was accessed through a tunnel similar to the approach for each window. He could see "FO" sitting at her mooring, and also drifting debris that he trusted would not damage the fragile floats.

The next morning at breakfast, Ward found Cobham in discussion with an army officer. Cobham turned to Ward and said that apparently, a tiger had killed an Army Major by the name of Pritchard-Taylor at a district north west of them and it had evaded all efforts to capture it. The hunt had been organised by Major General Sir Herbert Holman, the general officer commanding the district and apparently it had today mauled and killed a coolie.

Cobham told the officer that they saw a tiger by the river not far from their stop and was told that the officer was going to report the sighting. It was not known, but it could be the same tiger? As Cobham and Ward prepared to depart, an officer they had met earlier, reported that a tiger had been found and killed.

The Times Newspaper in England reported. ' Cobham realises he is behind on his timing for the flight, but this was due to the death of Mr.Elliott his flight engineer, but his destination is Australia and not India and he is not hurrying because, after experiencing the fearful heat and storms of the Persian Gulf, he desires to conserve his physical energies as well as the powers of the engine. He hoped that the return journey would be quicker. The worst of the first part of this journey, the most difficult stage, lay immediately before him and Sergeant Ward, namely the crossing from Calcutta to Victoria Point in the face of heavy monsoon conditions. The flight had shown the possibilities of using an air cooled engine in the great heat of the day The reporter then asked how Mr.Cobham felt following the death of his friend Mr.Elliott? Cobham replied, he felt less depressed than when he left Basra but is not quite well yet and the method of Mr.Elliott's death still haunted him.'

July 23rd. Ward, used the starter handle to start the engine, carefully climbed back into the forward cabin and Cobham took off at eight o'clock. He pointed 'FO' towards the morning sun following the River Ganges all of the way to a town called Hugli having passed over Patna at ten twenty-five am. Hugli is a suburb of Calcutta. They had been flying non-stop for six hours without incident and arrived at two in the afternoon, a distance of about six hundred miles at an average speed of approximately 100 miles per hour.

A motor launch was in attendance so Cobham taxied close to it having cut the engine, and Ward threw a secured rope, which was taken on board by the launch. They were then towed to a police launch that was to take care of the mooring for them. The first words their Calcutta friends got across to them were, that if they were to fall into the water they would never come up again! Apparently there were very fast undercurrents that could take anyone under and their body might not be seen for months. The water was very dirty with waste swirling about everywhere. Knowing Ward's aptitude for falling overboard Cobham warned him and they crept around their floats with utmost care.

They alighted carefully and boarded the Burma Oil Company

launch where lunch had been prepared. The station staff officer and the agent of the Burma Oil Company were their hosts and a merry time was had. Cobham related to the agents that he considered the flight was progressing well, and despite trial and tribulation there would be compensation.

They spent the night at Fort William, the army garrison at Hugli. It was a friendly place and Cobham decided that a day off flying should be beneficial. It was also common sense owing to his intense fatigue, but Ward was up early the next day, and he used the relative cool of the morning to make extensive examination of the aircraft before retiring for lunch and an afternoon sleep. Cobham found time to relax and did not want others around.

Ward meanwhile wanted to explore the sights and scenes of Calcutta so he got a lift in an British Army vehicle going into the centre and joined a few Army personnel for a night out.

The next morning Cobham and Ward inspected maps for the next part of their flight. Cobham had planned to cross the Ganges Delta from a point south of Kakdwip. He would then fly east to a point, ninety degrees, to Lata Chapli, and then fly to twenty two degrees north of ninety one degrees east where they should pass over South Hatia island towards Chittagong. They would then turn south along the coast towards the small island of Akyab, (or Sittwe as it was also known), where, before continuing to Rangoon, they will stop. (See To the Ends Of The Earth-Diary of Cobham).

Cobham handed a map to Ward and told him to expect bad weather on route, but he should put on a brave face! He said that they could not always choose the weather for long distance flights. He pencilled the route on the next map of a series covering the journey.

They had said goodbye to their new friends and, as the conditions were nearly perfect Ward, was able to cast adrift and Cobham started the engine from the self-start magneto, but when he pushed his feet on the rudder pedals he found that the rudder had jammed. Immediately the engine was stopped and Cobham signalled for the launch to take them in tow whilst they tried to turn the aircraft around so that they could work on the tail when it overhung the launch. The tail was too high to reach from the sea. The repair necessitated adjusting the wires travelling from the pedals to each side of the rudder and this delayed their flight by half an hour.

They left Hugli soon after and watched the sun rise gently as they raced towards it over the flooded plains of the Ganges Delta where the River Ganges fans out to feel the sea with finger like distribution.

Eventually, they passed over South Hatia Island and headed for the coast of Chittagong, slowly turning south east to cut the corner. In the distance Ward could see a huge bank of cloud shrouding the mainland. Into the tube Cobham shouted that there appeared to be bad weather ahead and therefore the weather forecast seemed to be correct!

Cobham flew 'FO' towards the far shore and then turned south towards Akyab Island situated off the coast of Burma where they landed four hours after leaving Calcutta.

It was a time to refresh with lunch that had been prepared for them at the last stop. This proved beneficial because the monsoon was gaining in intensity, but Cobham was adamant that the weather should not interfere with the flying program. Aircraft had to be produced in the future that would make long distance flying possible, and comfortable. So, there should be no delay for he had to complete the task!

19: The steamer

Ward carried out pre-flight checks after lunch and considered that 'FO' was ready enough for the journey ahead. Alan Cobham had a flight plan that was to take them to Rangoon. However, the monsoon was gaining in severity and Ward wondered if they should continue? He awaited the arrival of Cobham who was being briefed on the weather forecast by the cable office operator of the Army base camp.

They would have to push on to Rangoon announced Cobham when he arrived alongside 'FO'. He had been made aware of the intensity of the monsoon and the forecast was not good but he thought they had a good chance and hoped Ward agreed to an early departure? Ward reminded Cobham that he, Arthur Ward, was not the pilot, and if Mr Cobham thought they could make Rangoon without problems then he agreed to an early departure! By now he had every faith in his captain!

Cobham agreed to go over the maps again to make sure they both agreed on the route. He asked Ward to keep a good lookout at all times, follow the route on the copy of the plans and should he have any comments to make at any time during the flight just wave through the flap between them and above all, do not fall asleep!

Cobham took the aircraft out into deeper water and turned into the wind. With thumbs up signal he increased the throttle and 'FO' carried forward into a choppy sea and, at a speed of about forty knots, lifted the aircraft into the cloudy and rain-swept sky. The aircraft gained height as Cobham conducted a banking turn that took them in the direction south, then after a while turned slightly southeast along the coast of West Burma.

It was not long before flying conditions deteriorated and blinding rain hit the aircraft. Time and time again the wind buffeted the airframe and Ward wondered whether 'FO' would be torn apart. The Jaguar engine groaned as it pulled the aircraft through ever changing weather patterns; one minute the aircraft gained speed at increasing knots, only to be hit by forward winds that held it back. The aircraft gained height as suddenly as it lost it and Cobham's stubborn determination was required to keep the aircraft in the air.

They continued to fly south and finally, in one storm of great severity, and flying blind, Cobham lost his way and asked Ward where he thought they were, by shouting through the tube. He was mindful that the Arakan Mountain Range that ran south from India to the southern- most part of Burma was not far from the coastline. Ward shouting above the noise around him said he could see land at times below them. However, he calculated they should not be far from turning into the Andaman Sea towards Rangoon. Then he reported to seeing water again! Cobham, agreed, and said he would go down towards sea level to establish their bearings before continuing the journey!

Under the cloud base Cobham was able to see water and a steamer heading in their direction. They landed not far from the steamer that slowly made its way along the quiet waters. Cobham decided to pull along side and shout to them to throw a line, because on either side there were thick wooded areas that might be dangerous, if 'FO' drifted in to them.

A crowd of natives hung over the side of the steamer with wide mouths open but the Captain showed no intention of slowing down, despite arm waving by Cobham. He decided to fire a rocket and this seemed to impress those on the steamer because it slowed down. Cobham hoped that they would put down a boat so that the aircraft could be taken into tow but they were so slow at deciding what to do that "FO" drifted down stream and collided with bushes and trees that grew deep into the water along the banks of the river.

A native was put into a launch and came close to the aircraft, but he refused to come near enough to help even though it was obvious that the motor launch or the steamer was going to have to pull them out from the branches of the trees that clung to the banks like leaches.

The grimness of the situation was part relieved by Ward as he stood on the end of the float, in his best cockney voice, shouted a stream of obscenities until, Cobham with tears in his eyes, jumped onto the boat and signalled to be taken to the captain of the steamer.

The captain was a native who, like all of his crew, could not speak English. It was a large steamer carrying a cargo of petrol. Cobham showed the captain his map and asked if he could see the steamer's map but soon learnt that the captain had never seen a map before. However, he knew where he had come from and where he was going and from the limited communication Cobham thought he knew where their position was.

It appears that the steamer had come from Rangoon and they had landed on a stretch of water called Basein Creek an inlet of the Andaman Sea. Cobham could not find it on the map but, there was a Pathein River shown and supposed that 'ein' of that name might have sounded similar when the Captain, who could not speak English had in his language described it as Basein Creek. When taking off Cobham would fly north east to approach the sea, then turn north to bring them to Rangoon.

Cobham somehow managed to get a promise from the captain to drop anchor and stand by until his aircraft was clear of the bushes. He jumped into the launch once more and went quickly to the aircraft, where he jumped onto the floats. Ward was pleased to see him again because he had been busy keeping "FO" away from the bushes by using his feet to push off when necessary. A rope was attached to the float-stay and thrown to the native in the launch, who the took the end to the steamer.

Ward started the engine using the starting handle and though wet from the monsoon, the engine started immediately. The plan, when the engine was firing correctly, Cobham would open it up, and Ward would cut the rope and climb into the cabin as the aircraft taxied into the middle of the river for take-off. Within three seconds the rain soaked seaplane took off, circling over the steamer. The crew of the steamer stood aghast looking up at these crazy people who happened to drop in on them and left in haste after cutting their valuable rope, without a thank you.

The aircraft soon left the steamer behind and the information given by the captain allowed Cobham to redirect the aircraft by flying north east over several irrigation rivers towards Rangoon. The course took them over rice fields and a variety of crops, tended by farmers and bullock-drawn carts. The bad weather started to ease and the approach to Rangoon was made from the south. The journey from Basein Creek (?) had taken them to the inlet from the Andaman Sea and they needed to arrive close to the centre of Rangoon to obtain rest for the night and a safe berth for 'FO'.

20: Rangoon (Yangon) to Penang

As they approached Rangoon (Yangon) Cobham shouted into the communication tube for Ward to look out for the sacred Shwedagon Pagoda, an ancient Buddhist shrine that rises, 345 feet high(105 metres) and is covered in gold leaf. It is over two thousand years old and the top of the Stupa Dome is encrusted with more than four thousand diamonds, the largest of which is a seventy carat diamond.

Cobham landed on water close to Monkey Point that was being developed into a seaplane base near the railway station, and was met by an Army launch that directed them to a mooring.

One of the crew of the launch found it his duty to jump overboard and emerge close to the floats, at which point Ward threw him a rope. The now muddy man called for more help and with several men now in the muddy waters they pulled "FO" to the shore and manhandled it onto the slip way. Ward got out the small float wheels with a long spindle from the hatch under the body of the seaplane and fixed these to the underside of the floats, by feeding the spindle through special water-tight holes from one float to the other and then attaching the wheels.

There was not much clearance and the utmost care was needed to raise 'FO' up the slipway onto more level ground. The introduction of Cobham and Ward to Rangoon (Yangon) lacked polish or charm as all of their attention was concentrated on getting the native helpers, who were bullied into action, to hold or push the delicate aircraft in the right places. Any European around was immediately commandeered to assist and if he grinned at the situation, this was quickly wiped off his face by a rude remark from Cobham.

Eventually the seaplane was housed in the hanger, baggage taken from the aircraft, and enquiries were made about refuelling and cleaning of the airframe and repainting the floats for the next day.

Alan Cobham left Ward to complete the arrangements and was taken by car to his hotel where, after a hot bath, he was able to meet journalists to give his report prior to catching up on correspondence, completing the writing up of the daily log and sending off cables with instructions for other stopovers on the journey. Cobham had flown to Rangoon before with Sir Sefton Brancker and Arthur Elliott the year before so he was well known by the local authority.

Alan Cobham returned to Ward with drinks and asked him what he had found? Ward told him and together they set about making any repairs.

Apparently everything appeared to be satisfactory until after checking twelve spark plugs, the last two of the fourteen spark plugs were checked as faulty. Each was designed to ignite the fuel that was sucked into the combustion chamber to which it was connected. In each chamber was a piston that would rise and fall depending upon when the ignition occurred, which created an explosion to fire a piston. Each piston was connected to an arm fixed to an offset part of the drive rod and the combustion turned the rod a part way.

All of the chambers were situated around the outside of the engine, hence 'Radial,' and a series of combustions completed a full revolution. The propeller was connected to the drive rod and rotated several hundred times a minute.

On inspecting the last two spark plugs, Ward observed that oil was evident on each plug. This meant that a gasket, sealing the two halves of the engine around the moving parts, had developed a hole allowing valuable oil to pass into the combustion chamber from the sump containing the oil. The oil was necessary to lubricate moving parts and prevent them from seizing up. If it got into the combustion chamber, the oil would be burnt off but would also insulate the spark plug that would not work because it would be covered in soot and would not allow a spark to jump from the insulated core to the earthed outer rim.

The spares pack included new gaskets, which are flat pieces, cut out of asbestos type material into shapes suitable for fitting between the two parts of a metal component to form a seal, but with cut out area which would allow the free movement of oil . All that was needed was to remove the fixing bolts holding the components, take them apart and replace the gaskets.

The problem was serious but in this case was found just in time to avoid serious damage. If it had continued for longer, the oil would have become quickly depleted.

Work would have to be done. They could not travel that day. The repair work took several hours and was hindered by the constant rise and fall of the aircraft in the water. The work became more delicate as boats passed on a regular basis. Ward had set up a closely formed net under the engine in case anything fell from his hands. Eventually, they completed the work and the engines were ready to be tested. The aircraft was secured fully from the stern and when started the engine purred into action. Cobham was happy and the ignition was turned off.

After dinner that night at the invitation of the Consular, Alan Cobham, as always, welcomed the opportunity to describe the flight from Akyab to Rangoon that he said ranked among the worst for flying conditions that he had ever experienced. Flying in a storm of great severity they had lost their way and were directed by a ships Captain as to the correct route. He said they were carrying out the flight purposely at the worst time of the year to prove the monsoon offered no insuperable difficulty provided the route is adequately equipped and that aeroplanes are fitted with wireless sets to receive storm warnings.

Ward wondered if Cobham truly believed all he said but had to agree that he was an interesting man to listen to.

21: Penang

July 27th. The servicing of the engine overnight found that a loss of compression in one cylinder of the engine was caused by a broken spring. Cobham almost doubted this fact because the Armstrong-Siddeley engineers told him that a compression spring would never fail on one of their engines. Never the less a spring had broken and Cobham was thoughtful in ensuring that when taking spares for the journey, valve springs were to be included in the spares pack. However, he did not have enough, should all of the springs fail. In fact, he recalled only packing three and one was now used.

Cobham lifted 'FO' off the water at 7.45 am and passed over Moulmein at 9 am with an overcast sky. The weather became stormy later as they approached and passed over the town of Mergui at 12.45 pm, low and fast. They arrived at Victoria Point, the southern most point of Burma, where they stopped for the night and refuelled from a small motorboat that was brought out from the shore. The sleeping quarters were extremely basic and they were glad to rise the next morning ready for the flight to Penang, Malaya.

On the journey to Victoria Point the engine ran irregularly and on landing, after the engine had cooled, Ward found that six springs were found to be broken. Ward and Cobham went their separate ways to try and find replacements. Friends of Cobham were brought in to assist with finding replacements and they turned up with three sets of odd springs from an old Thornycroft marine engine. Then Ward found one or two pieces of motor springs and so all valves had springs of some kind. They managed to somehow fix the engine so that when revved up, it ran at maximum revolutions.

The flight to Penang, some one hundred and fifty miles from

Victoria Point, was without problems and Ward considered it to have been the nicest part of the journey so far. Cobham noticed many seaplane harbours on the way and made a point to remember the locations should they require to shelter on the return journey.

They flew over George Town the capital of Penang and headed for the harbour in the bay, landing on calm water. They could not find a mooring so dropped their sea anchor. They had arrived earlier than Cobham had indicated in his telegram and the authorities were not ready for them. Apparently local fishermen had often stolen mooring buoys when left unattended so the remaining buoys had been taken in to a warehouse close to the water for safety and only put back in the water when pre-planned. It took sometime for the mooring buoys to be fixed securely but it had to be done and both airmen had to be patient and await the launch that was to take them to the port offices.

Cobham always insisted that they should both be dressed in a proper manner befitting 'aerial explorers,' so invariably they would arrive, take off their flying suits and underneath would be a suit, collar, shirt and tie. Often white shoes would be worn. On this day the temperature was about ninety degrees F (33 C) and humid with a hazy sky. Ward took the opportunity to stretch out on one of the aircraft floats, and the gentle bobbing on the water almost sent him to sleep. Wearing too much clothing was having an effect.

Penang is an island in the Strait of Malacca, close to a narrow strip of land, on the western coast of Malaya. In 1926 it was part of Singapore and Malaya, and formed a colony of the United Kingdom known as the Straits Settlement. The British East India Company established a colony there in 1786. Until then it was sparsely populated.

In 1926 the main product of the colony was rubber, derived from the sap of rubber trees. In 1873 Rubber Trees were grown in Brazil and attempts were made to grow Rubber Trees from seeds. After some effort 12 seedlings were germinated at the Royal Botanical Gardens, Kew in London, but soon died. Some 75,000 seeds were smuggled out of Brazil in 1875 by a Henry Wickham and a few seeds germinated once outside in the hot country of Singapore. By

1898 a rubber plantation had been established in Malaya and other Asian Countries. Commodities such as coffee, spices, coconuts, rice and fruit were grown on large plantations for export. Fishing was an important industry. The George Town port was a distribution point for trade between China and India.

For Cobham, Penang saw the beginning of public functions, which were often the hardest part of a flight of this nature. However, that evening after the seaplane had been fixed up for the night, the Port Officer arranged to look after Ward and Cobham motored off with the Governor to Government House.

July 29th

They were late arising next morning and after a large breakfast they departed by launch for the seaplane. The fuel tender arrived and Ward refuelled from cans that resembled milk churns. They most probably were milk churns, thought Ward, who was, no doubt, starting to hallucinate, encouraged by the fumes from the aircraft fuel which rose from the filler cap of the fuel tank situated on the top wing above the pilot position on which Ward sat astride.

They left Penang at 11am. The journey to Singapore was over the most beautiful coastline that Ward had ever seen. The deep blue sea and dark green leaves of the forest were split by a white strip of sand that seemed to take them all of the way to Singapore. Looking down Ward could see the outline of a large moray eel and at other times he was certain he saw shark. Seagulls seemed to swarm up to 'FO' many times as they continued their journey.

Eventually the coastline of Malaya ended at the Island of Singapore. Cobham took 'FO' on a wide sweep to the starboard side and eventually turned towards and along the southern coastline. Several small Islands paralleled the shore and soon they were flying over the city of Singapore and preparing to approach the bay situated in front of Raffles Hotel. They touched down on calm waters and moored on a cork float some distance off the shore, but near the Yacht Club.

Immediately they were met by a launch crewed by the Ex

Servicemen's' Club who insisted on being their hosts for the evening. The time was 4pm and they had been flying for 5 hours.

The dinner in the evening in honour of the flight was arranged at the Raffles Hotel, where Cobham had booked rooms. The Hotel was rectangular in shape with a central garden laid out with small tables on the grass for afternoon tea, shaded by tall palm trees. Around the central area was the accommodation accessed by a central staircase. On the ground level were the facilities, including the restaurant and Bar.

Cobham carried with him a dress suit but Ward had no time in which to collect one when he left Basra. He never owned one. Cobham arranged that he be fitted out by the hotel laundry service Manager. On arriving at the function Ward was immaculately dressed in mess kit and Cobham felt quite shabby beside him. He noticed that Ward sat very upright with shoulders horizontal and learned afterwards that there was a reason for his stiff carriage. He was scared stiff that the pins that held the suit together behind his back and inside his coat would come undone. It was after all a very swift arrangement to kit him out and given the time scale the result necessitated some unusual action.

After dinner Cobham told his audience they had delightful conditions from Victoria Point in Burma and no difficulty whatever. He said The Times Newspaper would be pleased to report this fact, forever wanting the British Government to know that the journey was progressing well.

22: Singapore

July 30th. In view of the late night Cobham decided that they would have a day off. This was the first real opportunity for Ward to give 'FO' a good inspection and make minor repairs if necessary. But after lunch Cobham invited Ward to accompany him on a tour of Singapore. This tour took them walking along Stamford Street, named after the first name of Sir Stamford Raffles who obtained the Port of Singapore for the East India Company in 1819, five years before Singapore became a British Colony.

They continued walking through Orchard Street, which was full of shops, market stalls and restaurants. Singapore, since 1921, was designated Britain's principal naval base in East Asia and everywhere were naval personal wearing uniform. They arrived at an arcade attached to the cricket ground and continued to the sea front. In the distance, past the bay, they could see flotillas of naval ships and many liberty boats passing across the water carrying cargo or personnel.

The temperature at three o'clock in the afternoon was 84 degrees Fahrenheit and humid, seemingly too hot for work, but Ward considered he should get back to finishing the servicing of the aircraft. He left Cobham, who had to confirm forward stopping points by using a cable service at their hotel and walked to the Yacht Club to arrange a launch to take him out to the mooring.

The sea conditions were easy with calmer waters. However, it was harder to predict rain although this seemed to happen at about 4pm everyday in Singapore, informed the receptionist at the Yacht Club. On this day the heavens were kinder, and Ward was able to carry out servicing by checking oil and water levels, lubrication of the controls, and generally checked the fuselage and wings for damage.

By the time Cobham arrived at the aircraft the fuel tender was ready to refuel using manual pumps fitted to each fuel barrel. It was the easiest refuel that Ward had experienced on the journey. Cobham arrived, sat in the cockpit and conducted his own inspection from there. Then the rain started and both men prepared to close off the aircraft ready for their flight the next day.

July 31st

The flight to Muntok, Sumatra in the Dutch East Indies was not a long one, being some two hundred miles. They arrived at about 1pm and the flight was made in fine weather, the first since leaving India. But when they arrived it was raining and a strong wind was beginning.

They were met in the air by three Dutch Dornier Wal naval seaplanes and on landing were received by members of the British Community and Dutch naval authorities. There was no sheltered water when they had landed and the mooring was too far out from the shore, where the breakers seemed to be at the highest. After a while the mooring was moved close to the jetty to get what shelter was possible from the piles supporting the platform. The wind was increasing and the aircraft veered violently one way then the other. It is to be remembered that "FO's" wings were only made from canvas stretched over a light wooden frame and any damage done to them would seriously affect their flight plans.

Both Cobham and Ward were worried about the possibility of damage but were forced ashore by the heavy rain and the onset of night. They were taken to a rest house in the village, on a hill over-looking the sea, which would have been very pleasant, but for the rain that kept them indoors.

In the evening they were entertained by the British Consul. However, a gale swept the roads awash with rain and when this was reported at dinner Ward and Cobham asked for help, because "FO" was unpro-tected and would veer with the wind. At midnight, with help, they were able to attach a second anchor and the aircraft weathered the gale undamaged. According to Ward, at about 2am Cobham awoke the whole rest house shouting that an anchor must be thrown overboard as he was drifting. It took some time to calm Cobham down and to convince him that it was only a nightmare. Such was the stress of long distance flying.

August 1st

On the following morning with slightly calmer seas, they said goodbye to their new Dutch friends and, after several attempts departed a heavy sea. Cobham steered a direction towards Batavia. The flight was along three hundred miles of coastline that looked like the loneliest place on earth.

A long desolate swamp was bordered by heavy tropical forest, which was partly flooded by the sea at every high tide. There was no sign of life. The cloud base lingered over the forest line, leaving the beach area clear. There was no way that a flight could follow the cloud line for the cloud came right down to the treetops. Should the cloud or mist have continued out to sea the flight might have been impossible?

They crossed the sea to the island of Java, when the weather changed into a perfectly clear sky. Several fishing boats were seen and each had a single sail twisted at an angle to catch the wind that would carry them at a speed of about five knots, the best speed for trawling a net or fishing rod.

At Batavia Cobham landed the seaplane in the harbour. After taxiing into a small seaplane base in the far corner belonging to the Dutch authorities they were received very well. It was mid-day on a Sunday and they were in time to be collected by motor launch and treated to lunch by the British Consul. In the evening they were entertained at a dinner held in their honour where an exhibition of local dancing held their attention for some time. Ward especially admired one of the Javanese dancers who curled her eyelashes in his direction.

August 2nd

The next morning their route was in an easterly direction over the intensely cultivated Island of Java. Along the route they flew alongside a chain of mountains nearly all of which were extinct volcanoes, in many lakes had formed. Eventually they arrived at Surabaya at the eastern end of the island of Java where there is a vast expanse of shallow water. Despite the fact that the floats of "FO" only draw a draught of about six inches (15 cm) the friends of Cobham had placed the moorings for the aircraft about a mile off shore. This meant that "FO" had to be towed this distance to the aircraft hangers of the seaplane base, the main base for the Dutch East Indies Air Force. After being towed with two towropes by a motor launch they came alongside the jetty and were received by the Commandant of the base who had arranged a magnificent welcome.

August 3rd

The next day they flew to Bima via Bali where a volcano was in partial eruption. Ward tried to take photographs of the clouds of heavy smoke that the mountain was emitting but the fumes and the density of the smoke were too difficult to overcome and they continued on their journey.

The winds came from the southeast and flying on the northwest shore they were protected from them. However, as they crossed from one island to another they felt the full force of the wind, which whipped the sea into foaming waves.

At Bima the landing area had been marked in protected inland water and Cobham estimated from the maps in his possession that the lake would be calm. But, he had not allowed for the down winds from the mountain and on the lake it was very choppy. The landing proceeded to plan but the refuelling became a nightmare while the aircraft was at anchor.

To make matters worst, the fuel was delivered in sixteen-gallon cans, which Ward had great difficulty in manoeuvring to pour into the top tank during the swell. Cobham assisted and between them, refuelling was completed, but not before considerable quantities of fuel had been spilt over "FO" and into the pilot's cockpit.

That night they were advised to move inland to special lodgings with mosquito netting around the bed in each room to protect them from mosquitos carrying malaria that was rife in the village. Each airman had an ointment smelling of lemons but containing elements of medicine to help to protect them.

23: The Dragon

The next morning, their hosts insisted that they delay their departure so that they could see what the islanders called a 'dragon'. On an island named Komodo, which is due east of Bima, there exists a land lizard found nowhere else in the world. The reptile is pre-historic and can grow up to ten feet. (3 meters.) These lizards are treacherous. They live mainly off wild hog, ponies and buck that are found on the islands of Komodo, even humans, but will eat grass and other forms of vegetation should meat be in short supply. They sit up on their tails and can run at incredible speeds of about 13 miles per hour (20 Kmh) to catch their prey, which they tear to pieces with claw-like hands that have six-inch (15cms) talons. The venom of the Komodo 'dragon' induces shock and spreads many types of bacteria multiplying to produce blood poisoning. Their jaws will dislocate to devour large prey and their forked tongue can thrash out at a distance of about two feet (60 cms). They can be seen in a range of colours depending on their habitat. They are asexual with reproduction, meaning the female can reproduce without a male, if necessary, giving birth to about thirty eggs which take three months to hatch. The mother Komodo is not possessive and will eat the hatched young unless they can escape by climbing trees where they will stay for many months until large enough to survive on the ground.

However, Cobham and Ward did not have to go to the island of Komodo because the local zoo, in Bima, had two ten feet (three meter) reptiles that Cobham and Ward were able to view. They both thought the reptiles, officially lizards, were the most loathsome creatures ever seen. He mentioned about the reptiles to several newspaper journalists on the journey and the stories printed became exaggerated and recorded the length of the beasts ranging from fifty to five hundred feet long. They caused quite a stir back home. Only the Times Newspaper reported a truer size.

August 4th

Cobham lifted "FO" from the water at a speed of about 45 miles per hour in an easterly direction towards Timor via the south of the island of Flores and the island of Rotti. The aircraft was still battling a head wind and at a speed of about one hundred miles an hour and a height of one thousand feet they had magnificent views of the ocean bed and shoals of whale, dolphin and other large fish.

The sea was too rough to land at Kupang so they diverted to a small bay south, at a place called Tani. Here they found that the Dutch authorities had courteously placed one of their government steamships at their disposal. As they approached they could see the S.S.Gemma lying at anchor and close to the ship an anchored red oil drum with a hook on top to secure the rope.

Cobham circled around the steamship and he and Ward were surprised to see that it appeared crammed full of ladies waving to them. They landed and Cobham taxied up to the oil drum that Ward successfully hooked and tied the rope to the port float of their aircraft. A dinghy took them to the ship.

It seemed that the total women population of Kupang was on board the ship Gemma. The arrival of Cobham and Ward had made the visit a general holiday and by permission of the Commodore of Gemma, everyone was having a joy trip. The ladies may never have seen an aviator before and looked upon Cobham and Ward as super heroes as the airmen climbed up the gangway, fixed to the side of the ship, to be greeted by the captain. After the welcome ceremony, when many hands reached out to touch them, they were allowed to wash and change into more suitable clothing supplied from the ships crew uniform range.

Later in the afternoon Ward reluctantly, for he had enjoyed the company of so many ladies, went back to "FO" to prepare the aircraft for the next day while the 'Gemma' steamed up to Kupang to drop off the sightseers. The next flight was to be the longest jump over sea of the whole journey and it would take Ward some hours to complete his work on the aircraft. Cobham took the opportunity whilst on the 'Gemma' to get up to date with his dispatches and also to prepare information regarding their departure so that the Dutch authorities could inform the receiving station at Darwin by wireless, details of when to expect them.

24: Kupang to Darwin

August 5th

At 7am Cobham was back again in his cockpit waiting for Ward to turn the starting handle, so ignition could commence. The rails of the S.S. Gemma were crowded with naval ratings witnessing their departure. A stiff breeze had developed and Cobham knew that the wind would be head on once they were in the air. Otherwise the sky was clear and the sun hot.

Ward clambered along the starboard float until he was by the starting handle. He knew that, once started, the airflow from the engine would be enough to knock him off into the water. The wing controlled his balance as he carefully lent against it. He had to stretch up to turn the handle and this act enabled his full weight to be used to pull down and it to start the engine. All that Cobham needed to do was to throw the control switch and adjust the fuel intake at the same time.

Once the engine started the next step was to release the mooring rope. This Ward did by untying the rope at one end from the aircraft, pulling the rope through the loop on top of the mooring buoy towards him, untie the other end of the rope from the aircraft, coil the rope for use next time, and carefully make his way back under the wing and into the cabin. By now he was ready to sit back and after putting on his helmet protector, enjoy the journey across five hundred miles of sea.

Cobham raised his thumb to the captain of the Gemma and taxied out to a safe area for take off. The next stage of their flight was to be longest over sea and, for several hours, out of sight of land. As soon as Cobham had lifted into the air, the Dutch authorities at Kupang were going to inform the wireless receiving station at Darwin the time, and also the compass bearing that they were going to take.

Cobham had already received a long wireless cable from a Colonel Brinsmead, the Director of Civil Aviation in Australia, informing him that the Australian Royal Navy ship Geranium would watch out for their flight over the sea and if they did not arrive in Darwin by the scheduled time, they would take the necessary action. What was meant by 'necessary action', Cobham pretended not to hazard a guess? When Ward heard this he said, laughing, that he felt very secure with that knowledge!

On the deck of the Gemma a compass check was made on "FO" as it flew due south over the southernmost tip of Timor.

The head wind still prevailed and Cobham reassured by the fact he had the finest compass in the world, a Hughes Aperiodic, developed during the First World War, settled down to a long haul over the ocean. In order to minimise the effect of the strong wind, he flew low over the sea and although at times as low as thirty feet, the average was between fifty and a hundred feet. At times the wind veered by a few degrees but Cobham made slight adjustments to rectify the drift. After about twenty minutes the land disappeared behind them and a sea mist made visibility difficult. Cobham estimated that it would be another three and a half hours before they saw land again.

Cobham by now was doing calculations in his head as to the longest and shortest time it would take to reach Australia, but in the forward cabin, Ward was asking himself what would happen if anything should go wrong with the aircraft and the survival actions that needed to be taken. If they missed the coast of Australia the problem would be a shortage of petrol? How would the aircraft behave, if it had to land on the rough ocean water below? Cobham by now had reasoned that if land was not sighted by a given time then their passage was too northerly to that part of the continent. In which case an alteration to the direction would be made so as to fly southwest.

Cobham had been informed that he should see land a hundred miles distance from the Australian coast, but for this to happen the aircraft had to be up as high as it's limit and because of the extra weight of the aircraft he could only get to about 9500 feet instead of the designed maximum height of the aircraft of 14,600 feet. It should be noted that above 11000 feet Oxygen would be recommended for the airmen because the air would be too thin to breath comfortably. When it came to the time calculated, Cobham climbed to a maximum height of about 9500 but he could not see land! It could be that visibility was bad and a sea mist had hindered his observation?

Cobham shouted down through the tube, that they should soon be seeing land! However he supposed the head wind has something to do with a slight miscalculation! Cobham got to recalculating their arrival time and rather than alter course Cobham decided to stay with the course he had set. Due south! However he was not certain whether they had drifted too high up the coast and several times he thought he had seen land but the sighting quickly disappeared each time. He recalled that in the desert, mirages of some distant oasis often appeared to deceive the traveller. Was he experiencing something similar? Many times a discolouration in the seabed provided an explanation as they drew near to land.

All of this time the engine growled away perfectly but as the hours passed the petrol got lower. Cobham began to wonder how long it would be before it gave out. The sun in this part of the World travels across in the north but high and now Cobham felt the heat on his back as there was no protection from the shadow of the wings, that were forward of the cockpit.

25: Land?

At last a faint shape appeared in the distance. It was a very hazy distorted outline on the horizon that did not change in shape as they drew near.

He shouted to Ward through the tube that he thought he could see land that he hoped was not a mirage. Ward of course could not see forward of the aircraft as the engine was in front of him.

Ward shouted back, that he hoped that his Captain was correct!

The north of Australia is extremely desolate and a very lonely place and if the compass course had failed they could be stranded for days. However, at that moment, both men were enthralled at the sighting.

Cobham stayed on course and soon was over a sandy beach, with cliffs at the back topped by bush. He descended to about 1000 feet and this was their first sighting of Australia, and although not the area they were to land at, it was better than no land at all.

Cobham climbed to about three thousand feet to get a better view and reckoned that after coming five hundred miles over open sea and for much of the journey out of sight of land, on his dead reckoning compass course they had hit their target and Cobham recognised from his maps the area of Herd Bay some five miles on the starboard side.

They proceeded along the coastline going in a south westerly direction for about one hundred miles arriving at the harbour of Darwin and as it came into view they saw the yellow funnels of HMS Geranium waiting there to receive them. They had been in the air for six hours. Both men were very tired, Cobham from the intense concentration and Ward from the heat inside the cabin.

Before landing Cobham flew towards the harbour and over the statue of the late Ross Smith as a tribute to the memory of the pilot who had six years before made his heroic flight from England to Australia, one way only but it was a triumph.

The crowds who greeted them on the north shore of the harbour close to the statue appreciated the gesture. Darwin is the largest natural harbour in the world and has given safe haven for many ships during the worst of tropical storms.

As they landed a launch came out to meet them and to take them on board the Geranium to a rousing welcome by the officials of Port Darwin and the officers and men of the ship.

26: Darwin

After Ward had secured the mooring to a large concrete buoy, some distance from the beach, they boarded the launch to be taken to the reception on board Geranium and gave instructions for their aircraft to be towed after the reception into the beach ready to be lifted out of the water. It was to be given a thorough overhaul and the floats removed and replaced by wheels, to convert it to being a land based aircraft by engineers from the Royal Australian Air Force.

After the reception "FO" was towed to the shore and the small wheels and axels used earlier in the journey to move the aircraft onto land were again attached to the floats. Cobham supervised the work because he had been involved with Elliott in designing and installing this equipment.

There was, however, little height available to clear anything other than a flat surface and therefore the process of moving out of the water up the beach when the wheels started to sink into the sand, took some time and required careful balancing of the airframe to avoid damaging the floats.

Once out of the water and up a very slightly raising beach, a lifting frame was erected over the aircraft on what was found to be very firm sand. The lifting frame consisted of three long wooden scaffolding poles, one erected on each side of the fuselage near the engine, and one towards the front extending out over the engine to form a tripod and tied at the top with strong rope including a pulley wheel. The tail was lifted by several pairs of hands and then placed on a trestle standing square on the beach.

Now out of the water in Darwin, 'FO' is lifted using a tripod of poles, pulleys, hook and a table. The floats were changed for landing wheels for the journey to Melbourne and back to Darwin.

Ropes were then fixed and suspended from the pulley wheel on top of the tri-pod and a hook attached to pick up a harness arranged around the aircraft. 'FO' was then hoisted sufficiently to allow the floats to be removed and the special wheeled undercarriage fixed in their place. Plenty of spares for this make of aircraft were available in Australia, apart from the floats, and therefore the landing wheels and frame did not need to be carried on the journey. The completed process therefore changed the aircraft from a seaplane into a land-based aeroplane for the next part of the flight over Australia to Melbourne.

The floats were carefully towed around the bay to a quay where the crew of Geranium lifted them out of the water and over the decks onto a specially prepared railway truck, to be stored, painted and repaired if necessary, until being required for the return journey.

Meanwhile Cobham and Ward took off from the long Mindil Beach and flew 'FO' to a landing strip and hanger at the back of Darwin where a comprehensive service was to be carried out by the Royal Australian Air Force.

The weather was very hot with a temperature of about 104 degrees Fahrenheit (40 degrees centigrade.).

On the 5th August 1926 Reuters described Cobham's flight to Darwin.

' Mr Alan Cobham, who left England for Australia on June 30, arrived at Port Darwin after a flight of 500 miles across the open sea from Kupang, Timor. Mr Cobham is travelling in a De Havilland DH50 aircraft, the same machine in which he travelled to Cape Town and back earlier this year. So far since leaving England for Australia he has flown about ten thousand miles.' Such was the interest in the flight by the media.

August 6th

The next day was spent relaxing and attending to the aircraft alongside air force mechanics. In the evening there was a dinner at the Town Hall, overlooking the sea, given in their honour by the Victorian League. Both Cobham and Ward were amazed to be in the company of an admiring circle of Australian men and women, Aboriginals with their women, Japanese residents, and Chinese, Malaysian and Philippine men.

In his after dinner speech, Cobham explained, that the main object of the journey was to stimulate public interest in aviation and to show that flying was no stunt but a sound commercial proposition when properly organised.

Colonel Brimsmead.

The last hop of the journey from Timor via Bathurst Island and then due south to Port Darwin, took six and a half hours and covered five hundred and twenty five miles against a head wind, flying at times twenty feet over shark infested water. He continued that he had heard that very day that their hosts had been very worried that they would not find Darwin because, especially, they did not like the compass bearing that he set and could miss Australia. However, he had taken their bearing from the town of Kupang, whereas their hosts took theirs from the southernmost point of the island of Timor. But all ended well because their planned land sighting was at Herd Bay, which they only missed by about five miles. Such was the quality of the compass on board the aircraft and the good planning that went into their flight!

He had given his thanks for the kind assistance provided by Colonel Brinsmead, who organised and arranged the perfect preparation for their arrival. Everything worked to plan, and he said he would always consider it a very great compliment that the Australian Government had sent their Director of Civil Aviation, nearly two thousand miles, from Canberra to meet them!

'Colonel Brimsmead was born Horace Clowes Brinsmead in 1883, on 2nd February in Hampstead, London to a piano manufacturer Edgar and Annie. At the age of 20 he decided to migrate to Australia. His business venture was not successful and he moved to Tonga working on a Plantation. However, at the age of 31 years he returned to Australia and enlisted in the Australian Imperial Force as a private but soon was commissioned as an officer. He was sent to Gallipoli after his basic training and proving his ability as a second lieutenant when reaching the Western front with the 24th Battalion was promoted to Captain. On the 27th July 1916 he was awarded the Military Cross, but on the same day was severely wounded in a leg and evacuated to England. Being unfit for active service, nine months later he was transferred to the admin staff of the Australian Flying Corps headquarters, London. After several promotions he was attached to the British Foreign Office with the military section of the British delegation to the Paris Peace Conference. He was appointed O.B.E. and sent to Germany with the disarmament Board. Over the next 11 years he worked for the Australia Government, directed the growth of civil aviation in Australia, created the air navigation regulations, investigated new aerial mail and passenger routes and reporting on possible landing airfields, especially those connected with flights from England to Australia. However, in December 1931 at Bangkok his aircraft crashed soon after take off and he suffered severe head injuries and remained invalid until his death three years later'.

Cobham reported, that the next day Ward and he would continue their travels from the same airport where the late Mr Ross Smith landed after his epic flight from England six years before. They shall fly via Brunette Downs and Cloncurry, across Western Queensland to Bourke, reaching Sydney on Friday, in about five days! He thanked everyone for listening to him and for providing a tremendous reception, followed by a long applause from his audience!

The Chairman of the Victorian League thanked Cobham, and confirmed that all observed Cobham looked well in spite of his experiences.

27: Flying Australia, Darwin to Newcastle Waters

August 10th

The floats now off and replaced with a wheeled undercarriage, and after being given a complete overhaul, 'FO' was pushed out of the RAAF hanger in Darwin ready for the long journey to Melbourne.

The chosen route for Melbourne was through the Northern Territory, on to Queensland, and through New South Wales to Sydney. Then they would fly through Victoria to Melbourne a distance through Australia of some two thousand, three hundred miles. They would try to follow the telegraph lines installed some forty years before, but these lines were not easy to see from the air. They also followed the cleared tree areas along the path of the telegraph wires whenever possible.

Floats now off, the aircraft is wheeled out of the hanger for the departure to Sydney.

The bush below them following their take off from Darwin provided a carpet fuzz of a very desolate landscape of tropical Savanna and Eucalyptus woodland. This was the winter dry season when temperatures can range from 55 to 100 degrees Fahrenheit (12 to 33 degrees centigrade) with little rainfall. During the summer months of November, December, January and February the rainfall can be as high as 12 inches for each month with severe thunderstorms and lightening. Caution was exercised when going outdoors during these months. Flooding was a regular occurrence that caused great damage to a town centre.

The flight plan included a fuelling stop at a settlement named Katherine where the inhabitants, made up of Aboriginals and Europeans, in a small cluster of buildings, were very upset that Cobham and Ward would not stay for lunch. This was because the distance from Darwin was short, being two hundred miles and they were already behind on their schedule. Katherine was founded around thirteen gorges along the Katherine River. It was an oasis but the airmen could not afford the luxury of a stop in this beautiful setting.

There were poor maps of the area to be covered and following the 'Route One Highway' was proving difficult owing to the dense bush and trees below. Quite often the aircraft was turned back by Cobham to locate and identify the road or telegraph lines that ran alongside the main highway. Again it was necessary to look out for clearing in the bush that indicated where the telegraph line ran.

The area around Newcastle Waters was known for cattle with around 30,000 head at any time in 1926. Cattle were observed for as far as the eye could see and the sun was just setting as Cobham located the landing strip on a very basic airfield. After landing and taxiing towards a service hut, a car came out to meet them.

A passenger in the car shouted a welcome to Newcastle Waters and said he was the Postmaster and with him was Sergeant Wilson of the Newcastle Waters Police Force. Petrol in cans were hidden under the bushes and had been put there in that location because Sergeant Wilson had been worried that someone might steal them. The Postmaster said they were not sure when Cobham would arrive, but the cable said to have fuel ready!

Their stay in Newcastle Waters was an interesting introduction to the lifestyle of outback Australia for Cobham and Ward. Eventually more than a dozen men arrived who seemed very interested in the aircraft, especially the engine. They did not say much, as each man moved around intent on absorbing the sight before them.

Ward thought the atmosphere to be an unusual silence as he set to work to refuel aircraft. The fuel had been delivered in larger drums than he was used to and their new friends came forward, without a word, and helped to lift them up to Ward.

Later that evening they were to hear the petrol for their aircraft had to be brought in from the petrol station some twenty miles away. Cobham was very grateful for the service and told them so.

Turning to the Postmaster, Cobham asked if is was possible to get a bed, and further explained, as he had heard it said before, that he referred to a 'Shakedown' for the night? The reply was in the form, 'Of course mate' and their bags were taken out of the aircraft. As he stood with two bags in his hand the Postmaster looked at Cobham, and jerked his head towards the rear car, which Cobham assumed was an invitation to get inside.

He and Ward were taken to a farm and found a dining area made from a few wooden posts supporting a corrugated tin roof, with chicken wire around the sides. A long table ran the length of the room covered with linoleum on which were a dozen or so tin plates.

Alan Cobham reflected on the event and considered that there was an unnecessary amount of clatter in everyday life in the big cities. As he recalled later it was indeed a wonderful rest cure if only for a single night!

After a few minutes, four sturdy looking men came into the shelter, lifted their feet over a long wooden bench and sat down. The postmaster took his seat at the head of the table and another robust fellow dressed only in a string vest, slacks and a grubby apron, and doubled as the cook to the assembled, sat at the other end. Ward and Cobham used the plank supported by empty wooden fruit boxes on the other side of the table. In the centre of the table were three Tate and Lyle sugar boxes being used as improvised food covers, because underneath them were three dishes of food. As these covers were lifted there was an almighty rush of flies aiming to make contact.

The Postmaster dished out the food and everyone took it in silence. Each man, after eating his meal, handed up his plate that was replenished with more food by the Postmaster, without a word. After they had finished they stood, then departed in absolute silence. In a short while the two airmen were alone with the Postmaster.

He recalled they were in one of the loneliest parts of Australia and supposed they were as far in the usable outback as one could possibly get. It is a place where living is too hard for women, or at least it is allowed to remain too hard for them to exist here. The men work long hours and travel very long distances, because they are in cattle country, and the beef has to be driven to the cattle markets several times a year. Women would only get in the way! He continued that he had arranged to provide them with clean blankets and a log cabin where they should sleep very well!

Although they did sleep well, it was a draughty cabin with gaps between the log walls and it became extremely cold that night. They were grateful for the blankets. In the morning, the breakfast consisted only of coffee before the airmen arrived at the landing strip, started the engine and said goodbye to their silent friends.

28: Brunette Downs, Camooweal Alexandra Cattle Station

The next refuelling stop was to be at Brunette Downs, southeast of Katherine towards the Queensland border. It has the headquarters of one of the biggest cattle stations in the world. It had been almost impossible to fly without using a compass course over the Northern Territory, because, there were no definite features that a flyer could beam on. The terrain always looked the same and small towns were easily missed on the vast rolling plains. As there were no maps that were accurate enough to follow the only way was to follow car tracks that hopefully would lead the flyers successfully to their destination. They assumed that a fair amount of flying in Australia would develop a natural sense of direction.

They landed near the main house of the cattle station on a clearing when a car dashed out to meet them. After refuelling from Jerry Cans that were carried in the car they continued their journey to Camooweal at the Alexandra Cattle Station which was to become the largest cattle station in the World. At this point they had to decide which car track to follow because Cobham had a rough map that showed several car tracks out and in of the station.

After starting down one track it came to a halt. Another was tested to be going in the wrong direction according to the compass reading. At the third attempt Cobham hit the right track that took them towards Camooweal. Shortly he viewed a car coming towards them and just to confirm that their route was correct, Cobham took advantage of the level countryside to land near the road and ask whether they were on the right route?

The countryside was now without bush but a few trees were to be seen. It was therefore novel to be able to land whenever at any moment, and after a chat with the two occupants of the car they said goodbye, and as the car carried on northwards, Cobham continued southwards.

Camooweal is just nine miles over the border with Queensland and in 1926 was a little town fighting for existence in the outback. The like of Townsville, Cairns and Port Douglas on a similar parallel on the coast have been a greater draw for population. The population of Camooweal would like to be described as pioneers for the new Australia. Camooweal happened to be the northern terminus of a new airline Q.A.N.T.A.S, and Cobham and Ward found someone waiting on the aerodrome by a new small hanger to give technical assistance, if it were needed, for their aircraft.

That night a dance was given in their honour. Cobham pretended to be a bad dancer so did not offer his services. However, Ward took advantage of some freedom from the flight by 'Waltzing Matilda' through the night, including a romantic walk along a bush track with the prettiest girl at the dance.

It was a very happy gathering of wonderful people, because as Cobham was to relate later, despite the grim pioneering work and general hardship of the life they were leading, far from all of the amenities of modern civilisation, they seemed alive to the possibilities of Australia and were therefore the strong backbone of the great continent.

29: Longreach to Charleville

The next part of the journey passed over the mining district and mountainous area towards Cloncurry. It would be the first time since leaving Darwin that they would pass over hilly and mountainous country and it was exactly at this point that the engine of G-EFBO spluttered for the first time. Below Cobham observed jagged rocks and deep gullies when another splutter occurred. It was not expected and rolling the episode around in his mind, Cobham concluded that, with the sudden change in atmosphere as they gained height, condensation in the petrol pipes had resulted in small drops of water getting into the carburettor and affecting the jets for one or two moments. The problem cleared itself and the flight continued after two more splutters.

They landed at the Cloncurry Aerodrome that was beautifully laid out and were immediately surrounded by an enthusiastic crowd of spectators. Cobham was excited to see so many people but had to announce that after refuelling they would depart for Sydney, because they had promised to arrive on a certain time and date. Reluctantly he said his goodbye and pushed on to their next stop for refuelling at Longreach.

They flew over Winton and at Longreach they landed to refuel. The area and the vast flat ground looked brown and dried up following one of the greatest droughts the region had known. This was a sheep rearing area and increasing numbers of them were dying daily, not from want of water, because there were ample artisan wells in the area, but from starvation. Farmers were purchasing hay at enormous cost but unfortunately had to watch their life's work being wiped out because the cost of feeding could not be recouped through the price they got for the animals. There was also another problem, with wild dogs, that would prey on the young lambs.

The landing strip had been extended at Longreach to accommodate the large aircraft Qantas required to pioneer their routes in the north of the country. Here was also an area headquarters for Qantas where assistance was offered should their aircraft need servicing by workshop facilities that were first class. Next to the small aircraft workshop Cobham and Ward were shown where they were building a similar type of aeroplane under licence from the De Havilland Company, that would be used for mail and also the flying Doctor service that was just being established.

Aircraft at Longreach.

It must be remembered that Australia was being successfully populated and vast distances were being flown to establish contact by air. For example the flight from Darwin to Melbourne was over two thousand miles. There was no interest in developing overseas travel, at this time, but they needed long distance aircraft to cover the huge distances between cities in Australia.

From Longreach they followed the tracks towards Charleville, a town in south western Queensland about 450 miles (750 Kilometres) west of Brisbane, but very soon Cobham could not see the tracks from the air. Vast areas of forest lay below them and no landmarks were visible. The compass came in useful at that point. Prior to the forest area they saw large herds of kangaroo, who were driven into the area by the drought. As the sun began to sink there was no sight of Charleville. Below them there was only forest with no likelihood of being able to land.

It was a very long course to fly by compass. Cobham felt sure that they were on the right track but Ward was feeling worried by now and felt it would be dangerous to continue. The sun was getting very low. Any open area in the forest might be a good place to land but the aircraft could be damaged? Suddenly, without warning, they came upon the town with houses hidden in the forest beneath. Then with not more than 400 yards ahead they were quickly over Charleville when the airfield came into view, and without circling Cobham landed, and were greeted by an enthusiastic crowd. Many of the spectators had travelled by motor, along bush tracks for a few hundred miles to see the airmen and their, now famous 'FO'. The airstrip was on bare red soil and red dust was flying everywhere until Cobham stopped the engine.

The flight had covered about seven hundred and twenty five miles that day and the journey to Sydney, the next day, was about another eight hundred and forty miles, so they should easily arrive on time!

30: Sydney

The Town Council entertained Cobham and Ward in Charleville that night. Colonel Brinsmead and Captain Jones, who had flown on ahead of Cobham and Ward from Darwin, arrived at the same time having been delayed on their last stop. They were flying a De Havilland 50, exactly the same as G-EFBO, but with the smaller, in line, two hundred and thirty-horse power Puma engine. This aircraft was more or less the standard type of machine used throughout Australia on all routes with Western Australian Air Way, Larkin Air Route and Qantas. Each airline only covered short distances of no more than 300 to 400 miles.

Cobham and Ward arose early to see Jones, Colonel Brinsmead and a passenger, Inspector Howard, take off from Charleville in a blaze of red dust. They were hoping also to cover the 750 miles to Sydney in one day.

The next stop for Cobham and Ward was Bourke in the outback, on the Darling River. The land around became greener as they flew south. The farms, fed by water from the Darling River were divided into large cultivated areas marked out in blocks for crops, and from the height they were flying, looked like a huge patchwork of colourful patterns. There was only a quick refuelling stop before they were airborne again towards the small town of Narromine in New South Wales, about 200 miles to Sydney.

Cobham had been asked to land on the polo ground because the Aerodrome was being reconstructed. Landing on a carpet of green turf reminded Cobham of home. They were treated to a hasty lunch by happy townsfolk and departed shortly after, for Cobham had promised to be in Sydney by 5pm.

Following vehicle tracks was not feasible because it meant taking a zigzag route that would delay their arrival by several hours. It would mean they would only spend four days in Sydney where Cobham had much work to do. Therefore he decided to push ahead by flying over the Blue Mountains. It was one of the most beautiful flights of the whole journey.

They converged with the Blue Mountain Range at Lithgow, where the scenery was purely stunning. The airspeed increase that came with a strong westerly wind meant they would arrive in Sydney before they were expected. Cobham had been told to expect an escort of several planes from the Royal Australian Air Force, (They were formed in March 1921).

Ward shouted up the tube that he would like to take some photographs of the views and Cobham agreed saying he would like to do the same. So he flew around the area for some time to use up the surplus time and get a few photographs also. The photographic results, later when developed, were not successful however because the Blue Mountains gave off a Blue haze that produced a foggy effect. Cobham turned towards Richmond to the east where he thought they would meet up with the escort and flew about for some time waiting for the pick-up.

They decided to continue without an escort, to the beautiful bay of Sydney with wonderful inland waters. To the south could be seen Botany Bay where Captain Cook had first stepped onto the shore and considered he had discovered Australia. He was not fully aware that the Aborigines had been there for over 50,000 years. However Cook laid claim for the land as being Soverign.

Cobham recalls, they then flew back towards Richmond in search of their escort, but evidently they were too early and should have gone on waiting had not a single Air Force machine appeared, circled once and made off for Sydney. It was not until later that they heard that a few minutes after they left the area the real escort arrived with several machines but could not find them!

Before landing at Mascot, Sydney airport, Cobham had time to fly over Sydney and took a photograph of the harbour area. In this photograph the famous Bridge or the Opera House had not been developed and shows the ferry port with ferries departing to the far shores.

Sydney Harbour in 1926, photo taken from G-EBFO. Notice, no Harbour Bridge or Opera House, whereas, the ferry terminal seems to be operating in a similar way to the present day.

Arriving over Mascot airport Cobham shouted into the tube that there were a lot of people on the landing area. They heard later that about sixty thousand people were there to welcome their arrival.

The huge crowd surrounded the aircraft when it came to a halt. The police could not control the crowd and photographers at the scene were trampled underfoot. Once the crowd had quietened down the local Mayor of Mascot where the airfield was situated, south of Sydney on Botany Bay, gave a welcome speech after which the aircraft was pushed into the hanger for safe keeping, far from the hands of trophy hunters..

The Mayor of Mascot, receiving Cobham and Ward after landing at Mascot Airfield.

The mayor of Mascot welcomed the airmen to lunch, when they were able to wear their best attire!! The Mayor, Cobham and Ward.

A public reception followed in the town hall and in the four days they were in Sydney, Cobham was encouraged by his host to give lectures, speeches and after dinner thanks that gave no time to relax. Ward just followed and was so tired that he kept falling asleep. He said on many occasions, when Cobham asked him what he thought of his speech, that he must have dozed off! It was Ward's way of forgetting the dangers surrounding the flight by calming his thoughts to a point where he just fell asleep. Sometimes with his eyes open.

Sergeant Arthur Ward's Holiday
– Interview by the *Sydney Sun* Newspaper.

'Early in June 1926 Ward was doggedly fighting sand and capricious engines with a little band of airmen who patrolled up to 250 square miles of land near Basra, in Iraq, to remind the Bedouin Nomads of British power and prestige. Shaibah was the Royal Air Force base for 84 Squadron and although only about twelve miles from the smell of Basra, sand often turned the day into the blackest, mulligatawny night. It threatened to clog up airplane engines, for which Arthur Ward had a passionate affection.

Shaibah was a hell of a place, Ward would repeat several times, during his interview. The sand, damn sand, was there day after day, sweeping sand which roared around the tiny metal workshop and yet, out there Bedouin tribes pitched camp, lived on dates and brought along sheep with them. What the sheep ate was one of the mysteries of the East? Often Ward made five or six hour flights as mechanic/observer when not a tree or green blade broke the soul-destroying vista of sand ridges.

He told a story of a Flight Lieutenant and a mechanic who flew out on patrol from Shaibah and ran into a wall of dust, swirling sand, terrifying mountains of it. All directions and control of the aircraft were lost. They found the 'plane miles out in the desert with the dead occupants, still strapped in the cockpit. Almost all of their bones had been broken. Ward said, in a casual way, that dust storms happened quite often.

He said that a year of his young life had been "spent" in Shaibah. Then came a bolt from the blue, said Ward, which made for a sudden transformation. In greasy overalls, Ward, one day last moth, crawled from under an engine, in the little desert workshop, to be asked to join Cobham on his great flight. The journey would be the finest "leave" he would ever have and a "bit of all right". He was looking forward to getting back to England, but not back to the Sergeant Ward of Shaibah, although of course he was still attached there and he had one more year to serve in Iraq.'

13th August 1926, *Sydney Sun* Newspaper.

31: Melbourne

The next part of the journey was over the new Capital of Australia at a place called Canberra. It was decided in 1908 that a new capital would be built but, the First World War and then the depression, held back the development. However the foundations of a Government House were laid in 1926. From Canberra it was a straight line to Melbourne over the high country of Mount Beauty, an attractive skiing area. The town lies at the base of Mount Bogong, the highest peak in Victoria.

About fifty miles out from Melbourne a lone aircraft met them to guide them to Essenden aerodrome. They could not believe the crowd on this occasion. It was more than twice the crowd that greeted them when they landed at Sydney.

Cobham looked through the cabin flap at Ward and he looked back. They were bewildered. It looked like the crowd would break through the cordon assembled to hold them back. It was obvious to Cobham that the people of Australia were more aware of the importance of aviation for the future of the overseas Dominions than his home country.

Landing at Essenden airport, Melbourne, became tricky as the landing area became crowded with spectators.

They landed and taxied as far from the aircraft hangers as was possible and now the crowd broke through the police barriers and surrounded the aircraft even though the propeller that could easily cut through someone was still turning. Cobham and Ward were so frightened that they would not leave their seats until they were convinced that the police could protect them and keep souvenir hunters away from 'FO'.

The Times Newspaper reported. 'A crowd of about one hundred and fifty thousand broke through the police barricade to surround Mr Cobham's aircraft on their arrival at Melbourne which was the furthest point in the first flight to Australia and back. It was amazing, the feeling for long distance flying the people of Australia had, but of course it is a country that appreciates the benefits that flying will bring to the vast distances to be covered from one side of their continent to the other.'

Leaving the aircraft took some time because of the excited crowd of spectators.

It took some time for the aviators to offload their bags from the aircraft and with help from the police, who were clearing an area around the 'FO', Cobham was eventually escorted, if not carried, through the crowd to a room in the hanger for what was supposed to be a press conference organised by the Lord Mayor and other representatives. However, young boys were dancing on the corrugated iron roof of the room, so the press were asked to leave and to contact Cobham later, at his hotel, because the noise had drowned out his reception.

Ward appeared, just before Cobham was to leave, to inform him that the aircraft had been pushed into a hanger for protection.

The airmen were now to spend a fortnight or more in Melbourne during which time Cobham said he worked an eighteen-hour day, every day. He was provided with a staff of secretaries to answer the many letters that started to pour into the Mayor's office in the City. In all over two thousand letters were received that he insisted should be answered. He hoped that the reporting of his journey, back in

England, would also drum up similar interest with the British Government?

Both men soon realized, that Australia had taken to aircraft travel more than any other country they knew about. Three Flying Clubs were founded in the two weeks they were in Melbourne. These clubs were using the small Tiger Moth, made by the De Havilland Aircraft Company that Cobham represented, and had been shipped out by sea in parts and later assembled in Australia.

Lady Cobham received a telegram from her husband announcing his safe arrival in Melbourne.

Meanwhile, Cobham and his engineer Ward, were accorded a welcome benefitting heroes. The days were exhausting with lectures meetings and other activities. The evenings turned out to be similar, and a visit to His Majesty's Theatre on 17th August 1926 to see a gala performance of 'Tell me more' was the highlight of a punishing schedule. The theatre box provided would in any other country be reserved for royalty or heads of state. This time it was reserved for the airmen and their immediate hosts.

It was a glamorous occasion, being mostly a black tie event and both men were supplied with a dress suit each. Sitting in the box, despite the sight of beautiful Cabaret girls on stage both men dozed off for they had had little sleep since their arrival.

The airmen were entertained at His Majesty's Theatre and after the show had their photo taken with the cast. Cobham looked to be asleep, the leading lady had her hands on his shoulders and Ward was to his right in the row behind.

At some point in the evening they were encouraged to visit backstage and eventually sit amongst the men and women artists for a photo shoot. Alan Cobham fell asleep again and was not aware the leading lady had put her hands on his shoulder, whilst waiting for the camera shutter to operate. Ward meanwhile, surrounded by a bevy of beauties had overcome his desire to fall asleep. It was noted that all the ladies in the cast of the revue wore a brooch of the RAF flying wings in honour of the visit. Ward is in the third row to the right of Cobham sitting in the middle of the second row.

During the stay in Melbourne "FO" was taken to the Australian Air Force aerodrome at Port Cook where the engine and airframe were given an overhaul by Ward and was assisted by a Mr Charles Capel a salesman of the Armstrong-Siddely Company, the manufacturers of the engine. He was out in Australia on business for his Company.

Cobham, meanwhile acting as an ambassador for the De Havilland Aircraft Company, used some of his time to promote their products, in between lectures, discussions and other activities.

On the return journey Cobham hoped to obtain a speed record that would entail two flights in a day, including a fuel stop at midday. Flying from dawn until sunset every day, he knew that this would be too much work for Ward leaving him little time to attend to the engine in the available daylight.

Cobham hit on the plan to ask Mr Capel if he would join the flight back to England to assist Ward in the daily routine of servicing the aircraft. However, Capel was a big man and Cobham knew that "FO" was already overloaded and would become difficult to lift off the ground unless he could make weight savings. He set about discarding excess clothing and lightening up all around so that they could take the extra weight of Capel.

Time was getting short because they had to get to the Geranium ship in Darwin to reinstall the floats on the aircraft. It was important to meet the deadline set by the Captain of the vessel who was shortly to embark on a voyage to the Antarctic.

32: Adelaide

After saying their farewells to the many friends they had made in Melbourne Cobham steered the aircraft out onto the runway at Essenden and opened up the fuel intake lever to speed the aircraft into the air and onto Adelaide where they would stop for the night. The extra weight of Capel had little effect on the handling of the controls, however, and Cobham's concern rested with the landing and take off in the northern parts of Australia, where higher temperatures and thin air would certainly affect the lifting capabilities of 'FO'.

Cobham and Ward found Adelaide to be the most beautiful City they had come to in their flight. In almost every direction they found large parkland areas stretching as far as the eye could see, surrounded by houses. It was therefore with regret they could only spend one night there, as time was getting short.

After Adelaide, the return flight was to be through the centre of the continent, following the great telegraph route that runs from Adelaide due north to Darwin, through Alice Springs. Their route first took them along the shore of the Gulf of St.Vincent where they observed prosperous looking farms surrounded by cornfields. Then they flew along the shore of Spencers Gulf to Port Augusta, and continued inland by following the railway tracks that would take them to Oodnadatta where the train tracks would end.

The route to Darwin now consisted of following telegraph poles that cut through the bush and following sand tracks. It was not as easy as had been relayed to Cobham. Several times it was impossible to locate the route as the cables ducked and dived through the bush. Cobham could only increase the height of 'FO' to see a long way into the distance in front of the aircraft to make out the track of the telegraph line.

The wind increased in speed and they found the headwind to be in excess of 40 miles an hour. This prompted Cobham to re-calculate his petrol usage as it was possible to run dry before reaching Oodnadatta. During his planning, Cobham had anticipated this, and he had made arrangements to land at Marree to top up the tanks. The land was very flat at Marree with desert as far as the eye could see and Cobham was able to land almost anywhere. However, there were large areas where arable crops could be grown because of the water supplied from springs. Generally, any town in the outback grew around the supply of spring water.

Cobham landed "FO" on a convenient spot and taxied close to the town for fuel. On learning they had landed the town turned out in their numbers, some in their cars, and very quickly in that small outpost the aircraft was surrounded once again. After a few pleasantries exchanged whilst Ward loaded the fuel into the top tank, they left in a cloud of dust, blotting out those spectators on the ground.

On this section of the flight Cobham lost his direction and landed close to a road to speak with a passing motorist to find his way. It was at this area a passing cameleer and his team of several camels were carrying railway sleepers for laying rail track. Cobham spoke to the leader of the group, because it was an unusual sight and did so to confirm the directions given by the occupants of the car. The leader of the cameleers said his name was Bejah Dervish.

Bejah Dervish was a Cameleer and his group were known as Ghan. The present day train is known as the Ghan after him. He used his camels to carry railway sleepers to the rail site.

Bejah Dervish, an Afghan and a Muslim became very active in assisting the construction of the Railway in this part of Australia. Born in India, he served in the Indian Army and arrived by ship at Freemantle in 1890. In May 1896 he set about assembling twenty camels and with seven men set out on a journey to the middle of Australia on a Calvert Scientific Exploring Expedition where eventually he settled in Marree. This is another story, except to say that he and his team earned their living transporting wool and stores, and also transported railway sleepers, using camels especially for the construction of the railway.

Oodnadatta was a small outback town with a population in the low hundreds surrounded by 3000 square miles of cattle stations in arid pastoral areas on the edge of the Simpson Desert, about three hundred and fifty feet above sea level. In 1926 the Great Northern Railway created a terminus there. It was where the cattle and cereals would be loaded into railway rolling stock for the journey south to the greatest populated towns. The Overland Telegraph Line route also went through the area on it's way to Alice Springs.

They arrived just before sunset at Oodnadatta, in a terrain that reminded Cobham of Spain; with permanent sunshine, blue skies, hard, rocky mountains on the horizon and vast open flat spaces below. However, the north wind brought with it the high temperatures as the wind coursed its way across the hot inland plains. Cobham was again worried that the air would be too thin to get 'FO' off the ground, but after a pleasant nights rest in the Railway Hotel, they left Oodnadatta early for Alice Springs the next morning, before the high heat of the day. The character of the landscape was now changing to one of bush and pasture that suited cattle and everywhere, when in the aircraft, they could see those animals seemingly all the way to the horizon.

33: Alice Springs

The MacDonnell Range of Mountains came into view before the aircraft reached Alice Springs in the Northern Territory. The mountains spread either side centrally for 390 miles, three miles from the town. The highest point is Mount Ziel, rising to 5050 feet, (1530 metres), but there would be a gap in the range which Cobham would use.

A landing ground had been specially prepared for their arrival and the aircraft landed perfectly. The airport area was very small and unusual for such a vibrant town of about 500 people, because air travel was important to the development of Alice Springs. By 1926 no Rail had reached the town.

Alice Springs was famous for being in the centre of Australia and was established in March 1871 when the Overland Telegraph Line (OTL) surveyor, William Mills, discovered a water hole and named it Alice Springs after the wife of Charles Todd, the Superintendent of Telegraphs for Australia. The area adjacent to the water hole was where the repeater station for the OTL was established. Aboriginal people from the area, known as Arrernte, have lived there for more than fifty thousand years and their name for Alice Springs is Mparntwe.

From Alice Springs they continued northward until they returned to Newcastle Waters, having landed at a place called Banka-Banka to deliver a spare part for a resident's car following receipt of a telegram from the owner asking for a favour. Cobham recalls that the car part would have taken about six months to come from Adelaide, including carriage by camel, a popular mode of transport in the outback of Australia. To be able to land the spare part on ones doorstep, as Cobham did, resulted in his saying later that it was just one reason why aeroplanes are very popular in Australia!

Friends refuelled "FO" and Cobham presented them with a large ham because their yearly provisions were coming up from the south on a camel train and were already six months overdue. This was appreciated.

At the next stop at Katherine, the owner of the local hotel met them and took them to his hotel in a rusty old pickup truck. It was a bumpy road and dusty, but they found the hotel to be similar to the conditions they experienced in Newcastle Waters on the route south. It was a rambling shanty-style building built mainly of beams, batons and sheets of corrugated iron. The owner was an Irishman who quite accepted the life he had. His family consisted of six charming daughters whom, he boasted did most of the work. The temperature in the shade was 110 degrees and there seemed to be no hurry to settle them in except, to offer a cold beer. That was acceptable to Ward and Capel, but Cobham needed to rest immediately and said so.

The following morning their host ran them out to the aircraft, about five minutes away in the rusty old truck. It also carried the fuel cans, which Ward and Capel sat on, for the journey in the rear of the truck.

Cobham recalls that the bill he received for the meal and bed came to £3.10s0d. Their host mentioned he should charge the expense to the Government who he assumed were footing the costs for the flight. Cobham had to explain that the Government had nothing to do with his expenses that had to be paid out from funds he had collected. Their host tried to give £2 back but Cobham, by this time upset with the comments from the man, refused.

34: Darwin again

On the 2nd September the three flyers arrived at Darwin to see that HMS Geranium had returned to the port after a cruise to Broome. Cobham was able to land on the wide beach, as the tide was out, and made for where he could see men ready to take "FO" out of the water by using the scaffolding that was used to take the floats off. The floats were offloaded by the crew of the Geranium from the railway wagon over the quay into the sea on the other side and then towed around to the beach, to be fixed to the airframe in the reverse order of the outward journey.

The axle and small wheels were put back through holes in the floats and left on until the floats were fixed to 'FO' then it would be wheeled into the sea, the next day, and the small wheels taken off and stored in the aircraft.

After the work was completed the three men met with the Governor General who was on the quay and went with him to meet the Captain of the Geranium, Commander Bennett, who invited Cobham to have drinks and told him not to worry about the coming sea journey to Timor. He said, after Cobham had ascertained the course they would take, Bennett would stand by in Darwin until news should reach him, by telegraph that, they had arrived. In the event that news did not reach him, within eight hours, he would put to sea and follow the course planned. He asked that no sail should be erected as this might distort his reckoning for any drifting currents and might miss the crashed aircraft.

On the morning of departure 'FO' was carefully wheeled down the beach on the two wheels. However, when floated on the water it was found that the iron axle that passed through the holes in the floats had jammed, probably rusted by the sea water, and could not be forced out. The only thing to do was to cut through the axle that was two inches in diameter and push it out from the other side. Otherwise to prod and exercise more force might damage the floats.

A hacksaw was found and Capel volunteered to start the cutting process. This took a long time, and he dropped the saw into the sea, which was rapidly gaining in height and it could not be found. They had to get another that took time and Cobham's plans had to change, owing to new time for lift off. He had planned to fly from Darwin to Bima in Indonesia. However that would be too far now and he decided to fly to Kupang in West Timor, still part of Indonesia, but about 400 miles short of the planned stop.

Cobham had planned to do two flights a day, with from seven hundred to one thousand miles travelled continually between dawn and dusk, to lessen the distance in time between England and Australia. They took off successfully from Darwin and with a following wind completed the five hundred and thirty miles in good time. Likewise the following day's journey progressed without problems to Bima and after to Sourabaya covering about eight hundred miles, all in one day. The next jumps were from Sourabaya to Batavia and then to Muntok, a distance of over eight hundred miles in one day.

On arriving over Muntok Cobham was undecided whether to continue to Singapore without landing or not? He recalls having enough petrol on board but he feared that daylight would not last. It had also started to rain. He decided to land. Cobham recalls that the decision not to continue altered the whole course of the flight back to England. Had he continued on to Singapore they would have missed the worst monsoon storm of the whole season in Burma and might have been in England, about fifteen or sixteen days earlier.

(See Sir Alan Cobham's diary, "Australia and Back", published by A & C Black,1927 now out of print, but second hand available and the book 'To the ends of the Earth, Memoirs of a Pioneering Aviator, by Sir Alan Cobham, Published by Tempus Publishing).

After spending the night in Muntok they departed early the next morning and arrived in Singapore about 9am. After refuelling, Cobham had lunch with the Colonial Secretary and Ward and Capel uplifted the number Four wooden propeller from the spares store at the local sea plane base and stored it on the aircraft. Cobham was anxious to continue so, as soon as possible, he made his thanks and got back to the aircraft to continue the journey to Penang, with what was forecast to be perfect weather. But the monsoon was brewing.

When they took off from Singapore they were confident that they would arrive in Penang that night. All went to plan until, as they flew north, they lost the protection from the monsoon which the Islands of Sumatra had so far offered. The monsoon was now blowing across the Indian Ocean and the weather changed within the space of a few miles. The flimsy aircraft was receiving the full blast of heavy rain and wind that restricted visibility.

35: Bad weather

Down below the hue of the terrain changed from dramatic shades of green and bright blues to dark grey that could be seen through the dimly lit mist of rain coming out of a black sea. Violent rainstorms with howling winds that drifted across their course. A strong westerly wind forced the tiny overloaded aircraft towards the mainland and shortly Cobham had to climb high and steer hard to port as a huge conical shaped rock some five hundred feet or so high loomed forward of his path. Miraculously he managed to save everyone on board.

Cobham constantly considered whether to turn to the front of the storm or attempt to fly around the back. For fifty miles he was successful in dodging between the constantly changing shapes of the storm but at last he was completely surrounded and although being buffeted, was forced to go straight ahead through the downpour.

Eventually, Cobham shouted down the tube to speak with his aircrew, that by now were quite worried about the conditions outside of the aircraft, that he was turning back in the hope of finding shelter in a cove. And with that he banked to turn towards the shore that was just visible through the driving rain. Then the mist started to clear, so Cobham decided to turn again towards the north to continue his journey but the weather and the looming dark mountains and rock, just visible and forbidding through the haze, made him decide to turn again and find a safe haven.

Cobham shouted through the tube that he was sorry for the rough flight!

He was told by Capel not to worry, except he had woken Ward who had fallen asleep, with his shouting, He often had a snooze when in the air, said Capel!

After travelling south to avoid the worst of the storm Cobham decided to turn and try again to travel north, but after a few minutes found it impossible to fight the very strong wind and rain. Mountains and high rocks loomed, so he turned back to find a safe haven. Looking down through the haze that started to clear Cobham noticed a small island with sandy beaches, so he decided to land nearby and attempt to anchor the craft until the weather improved.

After landing Ward and Capel got out of the cramped cabin and each sat on a float to attempt to secure the anchor whilst looking to ensure the seabed was free of rocks. It was not, and looking down could be seen a seabed littered with a mass of small rocks right up to the shoreline. Therefore Cobham told them to get back inside and he would try to find a safer location!

Within a few hundred yards they found a small sandy bay and attempted to anchor again but on throwing the anchor into the water they found that the end had not been secured to the aircraft. Despite Ward wrapping the rope around an inter-strut the drag was too much and the rope came undone. Ward held on to pull the aircraft in but he was being dragged into the sea and had to let go.

Cobham saw what happened and steered the aircraft towards the shore. The engine was stopped and Capel and Ward jumped from the floats to pull FO up onto the silver sand beach. The island was a jungle of twisted greenery that came right down to the waters edge, so the lapping of the waves pushed the aircraft closer to the dense bush. Ward lashed 'FO' to a palm tree and Capel looked around for suitable timber to light a fire, for by now both men were soaked and although the temperature was high the overcast sky made them feel cold.

Cobham, was slightly worried by being on what he assumed was an uninhabited island, without food except emergency rations that would only last about three days. They were about forty miles from the nearest Siam mainland. There was a vast wall of jungle on one side and a sea of rocks on the other and with luck they might get away from the island, if the Monsoon rain stopped!

However, Ward and Capel soon made humour of the situation, got a fire started with the aid of petrol from the top tank, onto a piece of cloth and erected a sheet rigged from the trees to shelter them from the downpour. The sheet enabled them to top up their water supply as it ran down into their flasks.

Shortly, Cobham made a decision to move by saying the tide was coming higher and would soon touch the forest. He was also concerned about the floats! They were being continually bounced about by the waves and the tide and could be damaged beyond repair? However, the visibility was improving so he instructed to strike camp, douse the fire and prepare for take-off.

With that they all returned to the aircraft and turned it around with Capel and Ward pushing the floats to face the open sea. Cobham recalls that it was not easy to take off because the wind was from the west and blowing strongly and they were on the east side of the island, under the wind. This was termed as the leeward side. The pressure caused by leeward winds caused down currents and made it impossible to just aim out to sea because the aircraft would be forced down into the sea waves and might break up.

Cobham therefore decided to take off due north across the wind, and at the same time try to ride the longest way across the waves. It was terribly bumpy and at times the speed increased then reduced rapidly as the undercurrent dragged 'FO' back and then released forward. It was like being pulled by elastic, until eventually, with a hop there was enough air under the aircraft to pull it up, gain speed and they were airborne.

The airmen up front in the small cabin behind the engine, had shouted, " Well done Mr Cobham", because they had blind faith in their captain cocooned and helpless as they were in a coffin-sized compartment. They were confident in Alan Cobham and totally committed to assisting him completing the flight back to London.

36: Trying to find a cable office

As soon as Cobham picked up his bearings he continued through heavy rainstorms until arriving at the north area of the island of Penang, flying over the capital Georgetown. Cobham decided to continue on although the weather was getting worst and the strong winds continually battered the aircraft. A whistling noise could be heard above the noise of the engine, accompanied by a vibration that could destroy the engine. A decision was made to land at a place called Tanoon.

'FO' was gently put down on the water and then beached on soft golden sand in front of the village. The rain had now done its damage, and prior to being surrounded by a group of happy Siamese, one look told Cobham that the wax cloth covering, that had caused the whistling noise and vibration because it was saturated with the rain, was tearing away from the wooden propeller. The decision was made to change the Number Three propeller and replace with the new Number Four as there was no time to make repairs to the fabric covering.

They had beached opposite a police hut and although they had language difficulties, Cobham discovered there was quite a good road from the village to Tanoon where there was a telegraph office. There a message could be sent to Victoria Point and Rangoon announcing they were OK and would be late arriving at the next point of call. The telegraph was not sent because the telegraph line was down some-where, however, this fact was not relayed to Cobham.

Whilst Cobham took some time to go to the telegraph office the repairs to the aircraft's inter-strut was made.

The Times Newspaper and several British regional newspapers were reporting on the 15th September that "FO" and crew might be missing as no report had been received from Cobham for several days. Various rumours were being banded about; that the engine had failed owing to the strain of carrying the extra man, or a crash, when all on board had perished. However, they hoped only the weather had seriously delayed their journey? The truth was, Cobham could not be reached and he could not communicate with the outside world.

'It was on that same day that another report came into the offices of the Press Association, a group formed by several provincial British newspapers to provide a London based news collection service, 'The steamship Egra arrived from Singapore at Rangoon and reported there was torrential rain and high winds at Victoria Point and that there had been no trace of Cobham, because the steamship had been on a similar path and had expected to see them pass over. Several attempts had been made to communicate with the telegraph office at Renaung, which is not very far from Victoria Point but no reply had been received. It was expected that a search party would be sent out from Renaung to Victoria Point.'

In London, Cobham's wife Gladys was very worried, but she had been in a similar worried state before when he was travelling overseas.

Cobham, meanwhile was feeling full of hope, after thinking he had sent his undeliverable telegraphic cable and travelling back to the beach at Tanoon he decided that they could continue their flight to Rangoon immediately. However a rude shock was to await him. The aircraft was not in the water but was still on the beach, with the tide at least a 200 yards out from the aircraft. Cobham was very annoyed with his crew for allowing the aircraft to be out of the water for so long and not be able to leave quickly, especially as the sun was shining and conditions were ideal for the take off.

Ward and Capel had to insist that the reason why "FO" was still on the beach was to repair an inter-strut and this entailed lifting the tail plane to get under the wing. It was then that Cobham noticed water running out from one of the floats. A small hole was seen and may have been caused when they landed in the rock-laden waters of the small-uninhabited island. The float was punctured and may cause an accident at sometime into the journey.

This leaking float meant another repair job. Capel dug under the float into the sand so that he could work from underneath and Ward opened the inspection plate on the top of the float to locate the hole. By using a bolt and two rubber washers and a special adhesive, Capel pushed the bolt through one rubber washer from below. Ward then attached a rubber washer and two nuts inside, locking the parts to form a tight seal. They finished the repair by the light of a paraffin lamp just after sun set. That night they all slept in the police hut on makeshift mattresses, and were served with soup, stewed chicken and potatoes. It made a change from the food at the uninhabited Island.

37: A pleasant gift

At 10pm the tide had raised enough for "FO" to be floated. It was towed out into the inky black of the sea using two rowing boats and was anchored safely. On rowing back to shore a motor launch appeared alongside. An educated voice shouted that his employer the Governor of Phuket, who was also a Prince of the Royal House of Siam and Phuket a town adjacent to Tanoon, apologised for the late hour but asked if there was anything he could do to render assistance?

Cobham thanked the man, who was the personal secretary to the Governor, and was about to say they did not need assistance, when a huge hamper was handed down from the launch containing provisions and included a bottle of whisky and some soda water. Cobham was overwhelmed and touched by the attention and deeply grateful for such unmerited court. (See To The Ends of the Earth, by Sir Alan Cobham.)

It rained for most of the night and the next morning. However Cobham was advised to recommence the journey with all haste. A mining engineer travelling through at that time for the ferry to Phuket, said they should hurry to Victoria point, to take advantage of the lull in the weather that would only last the afternoon.

They departed, and after an hour and a half were at Victoria Point, having passed through two or three heavy short bursts of wind and rain. There was no one to greet them, because Cobham's telegraph message had not been sent. After bouncing about in 'FO' for a short while, and a waving of the arms, a launch came out to tow them to a mooring.

That night Cobham and his crew were provided with sleeping quarters that made a welcome change from the night before in the police hut. Next morning they were in high hopes of reaching

Rangoon that day. The weather was clearer but very dark towards the southwest, from where all the bad weather was coming.

The crew went down to the waters edge and shortly after 6am they were in the air again. The direction was northwest, following the coastline towards Rangoon, (Yangon). However, the further north they went the worst the weather got and after avoiding several clouds full of rain Cobham was finally defeated by a huge deluge through which it was impossible to fly. Visibility was reduced to near zero and the force of the rain completely closed off Cobham's goggles. He had to take shelter behind the windscreen as he turned 'FO' around, using the instruments for guidance, and occasionally look sideways to see over the side of the aircraft without taking the full blast of the rain. Then, as he turned, he saw through a break in the rain that the bad weather, which was to the southeast, was almost upon them, so he made a dash back towards Victoria Point. All along the coastline he had to make detours to avoid some of the worst weather Cobham had ever experienced. He recalled that sometimes it was necessary to turn around in circles in a well of moderate clear atmosphere until the heaviest banks of falling water had spent themselves and they could dodge through again. Many times they were flying blind at about 100 feet above the sea, not that the instruments could be relied upon to measure such a low level to the sea.

Slow progress was made southward, but the dread of having to land on the rough seas below kept Cobham aware of danger and eventually, after an hour and a half of flying south, Victoria Point was seen again and Cobham managed to get down on the water safely. Ward was able to tie up to a buoy by balancing on one of the floats. The launch was sent out again to meet them and take them ashore to go to the hospital where they changed into dry clean clothing kindly lent by the District Officer and had the doctor look Cobham over to make sure he was fit to continue when the rain had stopped. Ward and Capel were glad that a medical examination would be made of Cobham for their lives were also at stake.

Cobham now prepared his telegraph message to London in which he concluded that an air service could operate through monsoon conditions, for if they had a proper wireless service along the air routes, with frequent weather reports, difficult flying conditions could be avoided. He continued, in spite of the horrifying experience of flying in such bad weather, he would say it is not impossible to fly through a monsoon.

Ward was able to find locally some Copal Varnish and proceeded to strip the fabric off the propeller and two coats of varnish were applied to render the surface waterproof. But, the wood was very damp and it was hoped that the varnish would dry quickly and be successful.

Throughout the journey four propellers were used. On leaving England Number One Propeller was metal and originally fitted to the engine at the Rochester Works in England. Number Two Propeller was new and made of wood and stored in the fuselage of 'FO'. Number Three was a used Propeller made of Mahogany wood and covered with waxed fabric and stored on the aircraft. The number Four was uplifted from Singapore on the way home and the number One metal propeller was left with the RAAF Base Williams in Point Cook, Melbourne, Australia. This is the birth place of the Royal Australia Air Force.

Having prepared his report to send out to Rangoon and to London he was told that the wireless station was not working at Victoria Point. The following day was again bad weather so he took a fast launch to the mainland of Siam to Ranawng where he was told a working telegraph station would get messages through. Unfortunately the telegraph did not get through, again, because the telegraph line had broken down. So despite Cobham's hope of sending news about his journey the outside world still did not know of their whereabouts.

Each day the rainfall amounted to five or six inches and Cobham could not proceed. It was now out of the question to become the fastest flight from Melbourne to London. He would just have to wait for a break in the monsoon before they could recommence the flight. Meanwhile, he consoled himself with the fact that an accurate survey of monsoon conditions in Burma had been recorded and that the value of his report would be far greater than had they missed this severe experience altogether.

During the four days at Victoria Point, important work was carried out. Cobham was able to update his flight journal, prepare a report for DeHavilland about the engine and aircraft, and start some of the thank you letters he would have to send out when he arrived home. Ward and Capel were able to work hard on polishing the area of the propeller not covered in wax cloth, clean out the machine, reorganise the kit and overhaul the engine.

In addition water was getting into the forward cabin so holes were bored into the floor to let it out. The aircraft was wet through. It was now Tuesday and everyone could see the change in the weather. The barometer in the hospital doctor's office showed it rising and on the advice of the doctor, who kept weather reports as a hobby, they decided to leave.

Four days after landing at Victoria Point they decided to leave, however, on taxying to depart there was still vibration and Cobham decided to go back to the mooring and endeavour to find the problem. It was found that the varnish had centrifuged to the tips of the propeller and caused an imbalance. They supposed that the wet timber had not allowed the varnish to seep into the wood whilst drying and so a decision was made to scrape off all of the varnish and store the now bare number three mahogany propeller in the fuselage of the aircraft and replace with the wooden number four propeller that was picked up in Singapore. The number Three propeller would still have given service but needed good weather conditions.

38: The airmen had been sighted

The flight proceeded without problems and at about two hundred miles from Victoria Point they flew over a town called Mergui. It was a clear day and Cobham flew low so as to be seen and at that moment the whole world learned of their whereabouts because a telegraph message got through to Rangoon and then to London. It was still the 15th September and the Times and regional newspapers reported that their arrival at Rangoon was at 1.15 pm. Two different stories, therefore, of their fate were published in one day with the later edition being the information to celebrate.

The Nottingham Post sent a reporter to see Mrs Gladys Cobham at her West Hampstead home. She received him with a smile that failed to hide her anxiety. She told the reporter, she was very concerned about the non-receipt of information for so long a period. The reports featured in newspapers said that the airmen were lost somewhere in the region of Victoria Point. It is over a month since she last heard of him. That was not unusual when he was on long distance flights. On the last occasion when he was reported missing, however, she made him agree to send her word if he were held up. She felt quite worried. When he came home she would do her utmost to persuade him never to set out on another long distance flight again.

She continued that she had felt nervous about this flight for some time. Many strange things have happened. Her husband felt very much the tragic death of Mr.Elliott and it depressed him. Elliott was a very nice man with very cheery ways . But she did not want to drift into depression as she had their young son Geoffrey to look after and he took up most of her time!

Then came the message that Cobham had been sighted over Mergui and Mrs Cobham was naturally relieved. It had not been an easy thing to adjust to, from her carefree life in theatre to being the at home wife of her frequently absent and famous husband.

After Mergui the weather worsened again but not so as to stop the flight. Travelling for another four hundred miles the airmen arrived over the Burma coast at Moulmein and then crossed the bay to Rangoon. On the 16th September they duly arrived in Rangoon (Yangon) at 1.15pm, having travelled about seven hundred and fifty miles, in time for lunch. In London the Times Newspaper reported that the news brought immense relief to many people in England who had been following the flight.

The next day it was raining again and Cobham decided that on knowing the difficulties of flying to the next town, Akyab, that he should have a special weather report. He managed to send an urgent telegraph to a town called Simla, in India, some one thousand four hundred miles away, and an hour and half later a reply advised that they should not proceed as the monsoon was about to turn very nasty. In fact Cobham had also experienced a bad flight on the outward journey between Akyab and Rangoon.

The weather turned so bad that "FO" had to be towed up into a dry hanger on special skids to avoid damage to the floats. The hauling up of the aircraft into the hanger was as comic as the journey out. The coolies have a great objection to getting wet and these gentlemen, dressed only in a loincloth around and between their legs, always carried an umbrella. As they lined up to pull the aircraft, it started to rain down heavily and as the order was given to pull, each man raised his umbrella to protect his delicate body. Ward was overcome with bewilderment at this sight, and went along each line of men seizing their umbrellas and throwing them aside, while the coolies stood stupefied. (Definition of a 'Coolie' is that of an unskilled labourer mainly from the Indian continent).

The whole episode brought about convulsions of laughter from the Europeans who had gathered around as the order was given to 'heave'.

They were able to leave Rangoon (Yangon) the next day, and missed the worst of the monsoon by weaving around the worst parts, between sunshine and storm. Eventually they arrived at Calcutta. They were ready to leave the next day but the weather forecast for the journey to Simla was unfavourable. The next port of call was to be Allahabad, about six hundred and twenty miles ahead, but the storm that had passed them in Rangoon was now raging there.

However, the authorities in Calcutta informed Cobham that a bore, a large tidal wave of about four feet, was coming up the river and could cause damage to the aircraft that lay at anchor in the river. They were advised to leave the next day. Luckily the weather was fine and they were able to continue their journey to Allahabad, where they stayed the night.

The next day the weather report for the journey to Delhi reported only a few local showers, so they departed Allahabad. En route they passed over Cawnpore (later called Kanpur) the place of the great Massacre of Cawnpore in 1857 when Nana Sahib, the disposed heir to the throne of the Mahrattas, led a rebellion directed at the British commanded by General Sir Hugh Wheeler. Cawnpore was a major crossing point of the river Ganges and on this day the few showers turned into a major rainstorm which meant flying through ten miles thick of rain during which Cobham feared more than once that he would have to land on the Ganges. However he continued, often flying blind as visibility became difficult, often as before looking out of the cockpit sideways before they eventually arrived at Delhi.

Flying very low, Cobham tried to determine where the mooring might be but the fast flowing river had made it important to move the mooring buoy. He landed and moved to where the fuel tender was moored. Ward and Capel attempted to attach a rope alongside where it broke and the aircraft started to drift down stream at 7 or 8 knots. It was soon in mid-stream, with sand or mud banks on either side, and downstream there was a weir where severe damage could be done to "FO".

Cobham decided that it would be best to get the aircraft onto the sandbank and he asked Ward to paddle in that direction. Ward used all his power but the paddle broke in half. At this point Capel jumped in and swimming pushed the floats, and Ward also jumped into the water and did the same thing and soon they were beached on the sandy bank. Capel then ran ashore with the anchor that Ward prepared for him by tying the anchor rope to a wing stay and they moored securely.

The fuel tender moved from its mooring up river and moored alongside. It was difficult to fill the top tank because of the river rising and falls caused by the wind. However re-fuelling continued and they soon took off to Bahawalpur, with a good lift into the wind that now blew down the river and not across, as had happened on the way out to Australia.

Again, Cobham found the mooring he had booked had been moved, but a launch appeared and took them in tow to a safe anchorage. That night they were provided good accommodation and excellent food.

The next day they had another successful flight, to Karachi, down the Indus Valley. The civilisation here is one of the oldest and is called Harrapan.. The first of the cities to be unearthed was located at Harappa in the 1920s in what was at the time the Punjab of British India. The Bronze Age civilisation was about 5000 years old.

They arrived at Karachi in plenty of time for Ward and Capel to service the engine, check all controls and inspect the mainframe for wear, whilst Cobham was able to catch up on paper work, send off despatches and make preparations for their journey through the Gulf. Cobham estimated that as they were now doing five to six hundred miles a day they should be home in London within the next week.

However, on the following day after a safe landing on the coast at Chahbar in Persia (Now Iran), Cobham found that the lack of wind and ocean waves were unsuitable for taking off again. But after a few attempts a slight breeze occurred and the overweight 'FO' lifted enough for air to get under the aircraft and enable a full climb into a clear blue sky, for Bandar Abbas.

They flew over Laft on the Island of Qeshm and landed shortly after, on perfectly calm waters. As they landed they could observe the harbour with its long 150-yard dock, said to be many centuries old. The island is opposite Bandar-e-Abbas.

A clerk of the British Consulate, who was waving his arms, directed them to a mooring. The clerk and several native servants had been waiting several days for their arrival and had erected a tent and built a field kitchen.

The camp was situated on a high spot with beautiful mountain scenery about half a mile from a deserted and ruined Persian village. Parts of the island were often flooded at high tide and therefore any high ground was sourced which enabled a dry camp. The airmen were provided with a large tent. Inside they found a cool breeze flowing through and enjoyed a delightful lunch followed by a little sleep in deck chairs brought in especially for them. A nice touch thought Cobham. Soon they were ready to prepare the aircraft for the journey next day. That night the servants carried out the table and under a star lit sky prepared it for dinner, after which, and a smoke for Ward and Capel, the camp beds were assembled around the table and they retired for sleep and an early rise the next morning.

39: The heat

As soon as the sun rose, all three airmen were in the aircraft having said their goodbye and thanked the clerk for his hospitality. They were soon on their way to Bushire, with a perfect take off. The welcome at Bushire was well organised with refreshments and a fuel top up. However, on take off for Bagdad, Cobham felt the intense heat of the day. Also the engine was running hotter and climbing to greater heights to get to cooler air, was becoming a problem. To climb in the thin hot air needed more throttle for the engine to increase power and this produced more heat. The extra weight of Mr Capel was also creating a problem. He was a big man.

Eventually, after several worrying minutes, Cobham managed to get 'FO' to a height of two thousand five hundred feet where it was cooler and Cobham was able to maintain this height and to throttle back. Cobham's ambition was that a record be set with the same airframe and the same engine with which they had started, also including a world record for the longest flight with the same engine. However the heat was now a problem that could wreck their chances?

Instead of flying directly to Bagdad and because the time was late in the day, Cobham decided to grant Ward the stop he requested at Basra to see friends and give himself a rest from the heat. When they landed the temperature was 115 degrees Fahrenheit (46 degrees centigrade). They landed safely and were soon amongst old friends, having steered the aircraft towards the RAF seaplane base. The airmen were given sleeping quarters for the night and next day, after receiving more hospitality, they were soon on the way again.

The next stop would be a refuelling stop at Bagdad before the next hop to Alexandretta in Syria, on the Turkish border (Now Iskenderun in Turkey). When leaving from Bagdad, the heat and the overloaded

152

'FO' was so overloaded that Cobham thought they would never get off the water. But they did and the flight to Alexandretta through the mid-day sun followed the Euphrates. By nursing the engine and assisted by a kindly up current they got to about three thousand feet where again it was cooler.

Before 1918, Alexandretta was part of the Ottoman Empire but with the Treaty of Lausanne Turkey ceded all claims to Syrian land and Alexandretta became a province of the area of Syria, that was a French League of Nations mandatory which also included Lebanon (Britain got what is now Iraq to administer). Cobham approached Alexandretta, having passed over and away from the Euphrates River as it turned north. He skirted the Nur Mountain range and found the blue Mediterranean before him with Alexandretta below, and a sandy bay where he landed on a calm sea.

The British Consul, Mr Catoni, who was waiting in his launch to direct him into the harbour, greeted Cobham. Capel inspected the engine and Ward refuelled from the BP tender after attending to other inspections of the aircraft. They were taken to the Consul's house where they slept that night, two thousand feet up in the hills behind the town. Cobham recalls that the journey to the Consuls delightful house was the most perilous motor ride he had ever experienced and far more hairy than flying. He counted at least fifty hairpin bends and over hanging cliffs, with the car travelling at speeds of between fifteen and fifty miles an hour. It was a very terrifying car ride!

The next morning they were off again flying along the Southern coast of Turkey. They had arranged to stop at an island called Leros, which in 1926 was occupied by and governed by Italy. It is an island in the Southern Aegean Sea off the coast of Turkey and about 200 miles from the Athens port of Piraeus. The Italian Commander was waiting in his launch to receive them, as was the tender of the British Petroleum Company, with ample fuel for their next journey.

After a quick refuel and reluctantly, because the scenery of the beautiful island was spectacular, Cobham lifted " FO" off the water and headed for Athens. Eventually he landed on calm waters and moored the aircraft in the same location as on the outward journey. Again, Major Black of the Blackburn Company provided the hospitality for the night. Next morning after photographs with Major Black, including his Company logo, they took off for Naples.

Here the route flew in the direction over Corfu, and soon they were engulfed in a mist bank with high clouds above, but having reached the gulf of Taranto they crossed the mountains of Calabria, in Southern Italy, in difficult flying conditions. Cobham had to force the aircraft up to a height of seven thousand feet in order to clear the mountain range and to get above a dense and heavy cloud cover. Everywhere he looked, Cobham noticed clouds forming, but with a certain amount of luck he managed to feed his way through and eventually get under the clouds to the sea, when over the western coast of Italy.

The wind from the west resulted in reduced speed and suddenly the western horizon produced a mass of heavy black clouds with flashes of lightening and drizzling rain. Passing through the straits between Capri and Sorrento the view was dismal and not at all like the popular sunny location depicted by Thomas Cook travel brochures.

Cobham landed the aircraft close to Nisida Island or Islet, (meaning a small island.) It is about 450 yards in diameter and volcanic and one of the Flegrean Islands archipelago, just north of Naples. It has a flooded crater forming the bay of Porto Paone on the South West side. An infamous Bourbon prison was sited there in the 19th century and still stands on the top about a hundred feet up.

As on the outward journey, they landed on the sea and quickly taxied into the small seaplane harbour on the mainland side of the Islet. After a quick refuelling, again laboriously manhandled with small cans held up over the top tank, they were advised to continue immediately to the seaplane base at Orbetello in Tuscany owing to the bad weather forecast at Nisida. It did not seem possible therefore to reach Marseilles before nightfall, the original plan. There was heavy rain on the route to Orbetello, but when they reach the excellent enclosed waters of the seaplane base the bad weather eased, they refuelled, and were on their way again.

The journey from Italy passed by the island of Elba to the right and the island of Monte Cristo to the left. Cobham flew over the northern coast of Corsica and continued for about 100 miles over the Mediterranean to the French Riviera coastline.

40: A strong wind

Le Mistral is a strong wind, cold, usually dry and regional that comes from the north-to-north west in France and accelerates when it passes through the Rhone Valley to the Mediterranean coast. The weather becomes clear and fresh, but winds can reach speeds of 80 miles an hour (135 Kms) and often become jerky in action with tremendous damaging gusts.

Cobham noticed the change and the reduced speed of the aircraft as it was buffeted by strong wind. He continued along the coast towards Marseilles. The wind increased in strength as they passed Cannes and it was difficult to maintain a straight course, but eventually after passing Toulon, Cobham steered towards the island of If with the 16th century Chateau d'If fortress, built in 1524 to 1531 on the orders of King Francis 1st, situated about one mile offshore. The seas crashed against the rocky coast of the small island. Cobham then turned into the strong wind towards the seaplane base of Marignane to refuel.

He found the B.P agent waiting for them with a very elaborate pumping apparatus, and they were able to refuel quickly and get on their way again at 12.30pm to Paris.

However, the Le Mistral wind delayed their journey and it was not until they left the Rhone valley, heading out over the mountains towards St.Etienne, that the wind speed dropped a little and the aircraft was able to increase the speed over land. The aircraft, heavily loaded, was difficult to increase in height, however 'FO' started to gain owing to a great up current of air. Cobham eased the throttle forward which assisted the up current, and soon they were at an altitude of 5000 feet. They were soon over the mountains and with a lower altitude followed the valley of the Loire, cruising past

St.Etienne, then Roanne and Nevers, flying under the prevailing wind until Fontainebleau came in sight.

The unforgettable part of that flight was to Paris, because in order to arrive in London at a time and day planned, the wind was still against them so Cobham flew at an altitude of about a hundred feet over hills and farmland, because at the lower levels the wind resistance was reduced. Should the engine fail, however, it would mean the ruin of a spectacular flight, as they were some distance from the river.

Cobham and the De Havilland DH50j seaplane, had been through the most rigorous and sudden climatic change it was possible to experience, but it flew just as perfectly as it ever flew, with rigging intact, cruising at over one hundred miles an hour at the end of its third great Empire flight.

The dirty crew arrive at Sartrouville where they were offered accommodation for the night, laundered clothing and 'FO' was washed down in preparation for the arrival in London.

At Paris they circled the southwest suburbs and flew up the Seine to Sartrouville where they landed on the river in calm waters. In order to land safely, the authorities had closed some river locks and installed river-blocking boats, to deter sight seeing river traffic. Normally local seaplanes were able to alight on the water after weaving through the barges and other water traffic quite easily, however, the word had got out about the now famous aircrew who would land in Paris that day.

They refuelled and were handed a telegram from Sir.Samuel Hoare, Secretary of State for Air, requesting Cobham to arrive the following day at Westminster, landing on the Thames, in front of the Houses of Parliament at as near as he could to 2.05pm. This was a change of plan, the original being to land on the Serpentine in Hyde Park but that was considered too dangerous. So, the Thames it was to be.

The Times reported 'Permission for the journey to end in the heart of the British Empire was given at a special meeting on the 28th September 1926 of the Air Ministry, the Port of London Authority, the Police and the De Havilland Company. Plans for landing on the Serpentine in Hyde Park were thought to be too dangerous and difficult to police the crowds. The plans for landing on the Thames required regulating the traffic at the time of arrival, and these plans were completed at the meeting. The details showed that the public will not be allowed on Westminster Bridge or Lambeth Bridge, but there would be plenty of room on the Embankment and in Victoria Gardens. Mr Cobham would not be allowed to take off again as the aircraft would be taken ashore and dismantled and taken away. After the airmen had alighted, a motorboat would take the aircraft in toe to a mooring opposite the Houses of Parliament. The airmen would travel in a dinghy to the steps leading to the terrace of the Houses of Parliament where they would be met by the Secretary of State for Air, Sir Samuel Hoare'.

41: The arrival

The Western Daily Press reported on Thursday 30th September 1926 that 'All being well Mr Alan Cobham on the conclusion of his long flight from London to Australia and back will land on the Thames tomorrow afternoon. The phrase "landing" on the Thames may sound rather odd, but it is explained by the fact that the machine piloted by the aviator is amphibian. It is capable of coming down on the land as well as water.' Not a very accurate explanation as with the floats on it would have been difficult for 'FO' to land on land.

The Daily Mirror newspaper reported, ' The qualities of physical endurance, tenacity of purpose, and the knowledge of skilful and accurate aerial navigation, have all been demonstrated fully in the course of this remarkable flight, which will be marked as a "Red Letter Day" in the history of aviation during 1926.'

After a good night's sleep and clean and tidy, well as tidy as can be, given their exploits, the airmen departed for London after saying their thanks and goodbyes.

By now poor old "FO" was looking dirty and grease-stained as indeed did all the clothing of Cobham, Ward and Capel. They arranged to have the aircraft cleaned down as best it could be achieved as they also tried to do with their clothing. A room was provided at the seaplane base at Sartrouville and they gave their coats and trousers over to be cleaned, dried and ironed quickly, whilst putting on overalls to complete the cleaning of the aircraft. Next morning, after a good sleep at the base, all airmen put on their suits that were still slightly damp, but not their enthusiasm, for they would be in London that day.

At 11.30am on the 1st October 1926 Cobham lifted G-EBFO off the Seine and flew the small hop over from France, across the English Channel, then over Hastings and Maidstone to Rochester where the banks of the Medway were lined with people and all three airmen were astonished at the public interest. Then Cobham turned the aircraft towards the Short Brothers Aircraft Works, where the floats were made and assembled to the aircraft. On the banks of the river, they saw that nearly every worker at the factory had turned out to welcome them back to the place they had started from, and with the same pair of floats that they had built just a few months before.

Cobham thought for a moment that they should land to thank the employees of that Company, but there awaited a special reception at Westminster, so after circling two or three times over the Short Brothers factory, Cobham pushed up the Thames towards London. Above the roar of the engine they could hear the ships hooting a welcome as they passed over the Victoria Docks and down to Tower Bridge. It was the luncheon hour and many would be late back to work that afternoon.

Over Tower Bridge and all of the bridges on the way to Westminster, there were white faces looking up at their aircraft and every warehouse had windows open with waving hands. As they passed over Blackfriars and Waterloo Bridges Cobham looked through to the cabin in front of him to see Ward and Capel taking photographs.

After flying up the Thames as far as Hammersmith, as instructed by telegram at Sartreville, Cobham turned back, circled Westminster once more and prepared to land. As he approached Westminster Bridge, but lower this time around, he could see crowds awaiting their arrival. It was estimated later that over one million people were on the Bridges, embankment, and even on the roof of the GLC building where daredevils perched on the top of the chimneys.

Cobham lands his aircraft on the Thames, watched by about one million spectators.

There was a cross wind and the tide was out so the landing appeared to be difficult. Cobham decided to slip in low over Westminster Bridge at a height of about 70 feet and now it was 150 yards to go, then 100 yards and at 45 miles per hour he throttled back on the engine and successfully landed on the water beyond St.Thomas's Hospital. He was late; it was 2.26pm!

G-EBFO is eventually put down on the River Thames and was met by a launch that took the airmen to the steps leading up to the House of Commons. Cobham had arrived after a round journey of more than 26,000 miles.

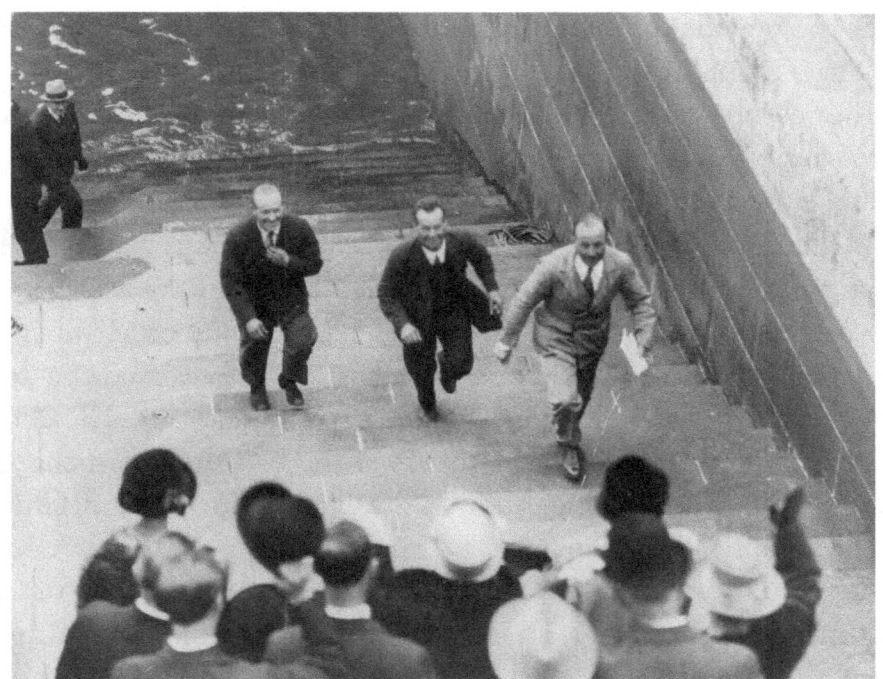

Capel, Ward and Cobham climb the steps to meet dignitaries, including Alan Cobham's wife. They were taken onto the terrace of the House of Commons (Palace of Westminster) where Cobham would deliver a speech.

Without further delay, the organisation to alight all three airmen went without a hitch. The Watermen of the Port of London Authority took them in a small motorboat to the steps leading to the terrace of the Palace of Westminster for the Houses of Parliament.

All three airmen, Cobham, Ward and Capel arrived to the steps at the Thames waters edge, where Mrs Gladys Cobham was waiting to welcome home her pioneer aviator husband. Cobham had a few tears when he saw his wife. Whilst it was only three months in making the journey to Australia and back, it had been a long time to be away, and he knew it was especially stressful for Gladys when he was assumed lost on the return journey.

Now he was to be with Gladys again but he had to prepare to meet the Members of Parliament first where he would recall his story of what the benefits of long distant flying would give to keeping His Majesty's Dominions of the British Empire closer.

They climbed up the Palace landing steps, so rarely used since they were built, then on to the Terrace of the House of Commons led by several Policemen.

The leader of the House Mr James H Whiteley was waiting there for the airmen at the top of the steps ready to escort the travellers to the reception on the Terrace. They passed by a group of Members of Parliament and guests, held back by a barrier, and reached the door into the House where a table and chairs were laid out. The chairs were to be used by a mix of Members of the British Parliament and guests that included King Abdulla the First of Jordan and Crown Prince Hirohito, of Japan.

Also there was Sir Samuel Hoare, Secretary of State for Air and Sir Sefton Brancker, Director of Civil Aviation all waiting to receive them. Also there was one who so desperately believed in the part that Aviation could play in bringing the British Empire closer, Sir Charles Wakefield. In attendance the great plane maker, Captain de Havilland, who designed the aircraft that had brought the three men to this location. He was more than pleased to see the triumphant airmen, for he had employed Cobham since 1921 as the first test pilot for his newly formed de Havilland Aeroplane Company.

The Lord Chamberlain, the Earl of Airlie, then officially welcomed the airmen and Alan Cobham was invited to make a short speech about their exploits.

Surrounded by Cabinet members of the British Government, members of Parliament, and guests, Cobham said that they had travelled 26,000 miles or more in about three months with the same airframe and engine. The purpose of the flight was to prove the benefits of long distance air travel to the future prosperity of Britain.

Cobham said he had travelled more than 26000 miles in about three months with the same airframe and engine. With our aircrew, Mr Elliott who tragically died in Basra, Mr Ward, a Cockney like himself who was loaned to him by The Royal Air Force and took over from Mr.Elliott, and Mr Capel of the Armstrong Siddeley Company who joined in Australia and pointed to the two crew airmen, to introduce them.

He continued, that the purpose of the flight was to prove the benefits that long distance air travel can bring to the future prosperity of Britain, and also to bringing closer His Majesty's dominions. He said the flight encountered many obstacles, that overcoming them provided important research information for planning routes and aircraft design possibilities for future flights. He recommend that the British Government took notice and asked they should provide the backing required to take matters further. He thanked the assembled listeners and concluded by saying that his engineers were just as important to the success of the journey as was the pilot. Applause came from the assembled listeners.

The sight of their baggy and rumpled clothing would never have won a fashion show. Indeed, the fact that Alan Cobham always wore a suit when being part of anything to do with flying proved to be the most unsuitable attire. You could not change the man and his habit, which was born from wanting always to be accepted in any company, and not to be caught out by wearing working clothes more acceptable for the job.

At the close of that day Cobham went to bed convinced that at last, in the year 1926, the public realised the importance of aviation to every Briton.

The birth of inter continental flights began that day. A journey that took three months, a hundred years later takes less than twenty-four hours.

And what happened to G-EBFO, 'FO', Built in 1924, by the de Havilland Aircraft Company, re-designated DH50J, the J being for the Jaguar Radial engine? It ended its life in Australia, being purchased by Western Australian Airways. Fitted with a 300 hp ADC Nimbus engine and new wings, it was used for the postal service in Perth and ended its days in 1934, ten years after being made.

THE END

Epilogue and Endnotes

Alan Cobham was Knighted and awarded the Air Force Cross on his return from Australia. He continued to promote seaplane travel for up to five years. His Flying Circus continued into the 1930's both in the United Kingdom and overseas. His interest in flight refuelling in 1934 was to use up his energy for the rest of his life. The Company he founded, Cobham Industries PLC, is a major supplier to the military in many countries and was a FTSE top 250 Public Company, now USA owned..

Sergeant Ward received the Air Force Medal, was promoted to Flight Lieutenant and made the Royal Air Force his career, retiring as a Squadron Leader in charge of training RAF apprentices.

Mr. Capel was awarded the Medal of the British Empire.

1. See "Australia and Back" by Sir Alan Cobham, published by A & C Black 1927. No longer in print but Second hand copies exist. (Reproduced as the diary of the flight, and also the flight to South Africa and Back, in one book. 'To the ends of the earth' published by Tempus Publishing 2007.

2. See Cobham, the Flying Years by Colin Cruddas, published by Chalford Publishing Co.Ltd, Stroud, GL6 8NX . UK. Published in 1997. ISBN 0 7524 0781 3.

3. (See Wikipedia. deHavilland DH50 aircraft, number built 38, primary users Qantus and Imperial Airways. Some of the wartime DH9's, the model that developed into the DH 50, were manufactured by the Westland Aircraft Company under license.

4. See 1919 England to Australia, by Wikepedia, regarding how dangerous the journey was at that time.

5. Not much is known about Mr Capel who joined Sir Alan on the return journey.

6. Royal Air Force Museum Colindale, Hendon, London NW1, acquired photographs and memorabilia of Sir Alan Cobham's collection. An exhibition in his memory of the historic flight was organised at the RAF Museum in 2014 to the memory and achievements of Sir Alan Cobham.

7. The Newspaper Archives, Colindale, Hendon, London NW1 - June to November 1926. (Now moved to Kings Cross, London.)

8. Wikepedia and Google to gain information about the fuelling stops. Wikepedia is charitable benevolent Internet Company in the Public Domain.

9. The Press Association, PA Media Group, 3rd Floor, The Point, 37 N Wharf Road, Paddington, London. W2 1AF, UK.

On the 5th August 1926 Reuters described Cobham's 10,000 mile flight to Darwin-

'Mr Alan Cobham, who left England for Australia on June 30, arrived at Port Darwin after a flight of 500 miles across the open sea from Kupang (Timor). Mr Cobham is travelling in a De Havilland DH50 aircraft, the same machine in which he travelled to Cape Town and back earlier this year. So far since leaving England for Australia he has flown about ten thousand miles. Cobham looked worn and weary and his right hand was bandaged in consequence of an accident with his machine. He made an extremely good landing on his arrival today, (Thursday) encircling the Australian ship "Geranium" in the smooth water outside the "Heads". A rousing reception was given on his arrival without incident. The floats of this seaplane are to be changed for a land under carriage in order that he may fly to Melbourne and back to Darwin across country. The journey to Melbourne from Darwin is about 2300 miles', reported the correspondent for Reuters News Agency.

10. On only three previous occasions have aircraft alighted on the Thames at Westminster. During 1921 experiments were carried out with the Napier Viking amphibian with the view to establishing an airport on the Thames, but the scheme was considered unsatisfactory. The pilot of one landing said there was plenty of room to alight

but the approach had to come in low over the bridges which invariably had traffic including double decker buses on it. No records exist
regarding the other two landings.

11. See www.britishpathe.com/asset/168156

Triumph for British aviation- great welcome for Alan Cobham
home again after his wonderful flight to Australia and back to
England 26,000 miles and landing on the Thames.

www.ingramcontent.com/pod-product-compliance
Lightning Source LLC
Chambersburg PA
CBHW051140020726
47501CB00005B/1606